DIVINATIONS AND THE DISAPPEARING DEAD

A WILLIAMS WITCH MYSTERY
BOOK THREE

ELOISE EVERHART

PB ISBN: 978-1-962759-02-1

Author: Eloise Everhart

Editors: Rashida Breen and Stefanie Spangler-Buswell

Cover design by GetCovers

CHAPTER 1

I huddled with my daughter, Grace, on our short walk from the car to the front door of the Bizzy Bean. I looped my arm around her shoulder as the chill winter air creeped in at the edges of our coats and peered up at the window display as we approached. Heather had updated it at the beginning of the week. It now featured Star, Heather's white-and-caramel-colored cat, peeking out between the branches of a Christmas tree, with a bright-red ornament above her head, her blue eyes crossed, staring at it. The ever-evolving window art always put a smile on my face. I grinned as I pushed open the front door, and the scent of honey roasted coffee filled my nose.

Heather glanced up from her place from behind the counter, her red hair tied back in a sleek ponytail. "Hey, Dani. I've got a few more things to take care of. You mind waiting a few minutes?"

I nodded and closed the door behind us. After two seconds, sweat pooled between my shoulder blades as the warmth from the heater washed over me. I shrugged out of my coat and made my way over to the counter. "You need a hand with anything?"

Heather shook her head and jerked it toward the table with the Retirees. "If we interrupted them now, Betty would never let me hear the end of it." The Retirees sat in a line behind the plexiglass cat enclosure, with rows upon rows of gift bags and name tags shuffling back and forth between the three of them as they skillfully put them together like a well-oiled machine. They were alone in the room. The newest batch of foster cats had already been gathered up and put to bed for the night in the kitten room.

My heart was full as they worked. Steven Bishop had roped Heather into helping with his latest attempt to revitalize the downtown. While not officially sworn in as mayor yet, he was still hard at work organizing winter internship opportunities for local students who couldn't go home for the holidays, all in an effort to keep downtown busy through the holidays. For the last week, Heather had radiated nervous energy. It was really sweet for the Retirees to step in and lend a hand.

Grace hovered a few feet from their table, her jaw clenched and her shoulders square. Her dark-brown hair poked out from under her Gonzaga University beanie. Her facial expression almost matched the glowering bulldog. I tried to catch her eye, but she pointedly looked away from me. It had been almost a month since we'd asked Betty to help suppress her powers. Her nightmares were getting worse, and I couldn't do anything about it. Every night, she dreamt of a woman screaming. If she hadn't already dropped out of university, she would have had to from lack of sleep.

For the past three weeks, the Retirees had found almost any excuse to leave whenever Grace showed up. Last week, when she'd tried to follow them on their power walk around town, they had picked up speed, their gray-and-white hair flying behind them. If I weren't so worried about her, I would have laughed. Until now, I didn't think there was anything Betty and company couldn't face down. They had apparently found their match in Grace.

"Just take a seat," Heather said. "I've got to finish counting out the till, and then we can get out of here."

I nodded and walked toward Grace. I slipped my hand around her arm, but she shrugged me off and strode toward Betty.

"So, when are you going to do it?" she asked between gritted teeth.

Betty faltered as Agnes handed the next bag down the line. She dropped it onto the table, scattering its contents. "Now's not a great time," she said as her hand darted out across the table to capture a stress ball that rolled away from her toward the edge of the table.

"You said that the last few times I've tried to talk to you." Grace leaned forward, her gloved hands splayed over the tabletop. Her ability to pick up the emotional resonance of an object by touch intensified by the day. For over a week, she'd been overwhelmed any time she touched something without gloves on. "Are you going to help me or not?"

"I'm working on it—" Agnes began.

"Then what's taking so long? I am losing my mind. I can't sleep for more than an hour at a time."

Betty cut in. "The thing is—"

"Another excuse? Is this a promise you can't keep?" The dreams had left her on edge. She hadn't been a moody teen, not until recently.

I stepped in and placed my hand on Grace's shoulder. "They didn't promise. They said they would try." I stared into Agnes's eyes, holding her gaze. "And you are going to try, aren't you?"

"I…" She opened and closed her mouth. "I don't entirely know how Mel did it."

It was always strange hearing people call my grandmother by her first name. To me, she had always been Gran.

Grace slumped.

Agnes reached out, her hand hovering over Grace's. "I have some ideas, things we can do that might help."

"Like what?" Grace asked.

Agnes took her hand back as Heather sidled up next to us. "All done. Are you ladies ready to go?"

Sarah nodded as she picked up the next card in the pile. "Got two more name tags to go."

Heather reached out to pick up the last one, but Sarah batted her hand away, and Agnes snatched it out from between them. She slipped the card into the name tag holder then slid it neatly into the stack. "And we are done."

"This conversation isn't over." Grace hugged herself and glowered at them before turning on her heel and stomping off. She yanked open the front door and stalked outside.

Heather raised her eyebrows at me. I opened my mouth to speak, but Betty cut in before any words could leave my mouth.

"We should head out. Don't want to be late."

We piled the gift bags and name tags into boxes and carried them out of the café. Grace stood waiting half a block down. Her arms remained crossed, but now it was mostly from the cold. She stamped her feet to keep warm until we caught up.

We walked toward the pier, the boxes clutched to our chests. The Retirees chattered with each other as we walked, each one practically talking over the other. It was hard to keep track of their conversation. I stepped to the side to walk between Heather and Grace.

"Was it a mistake to have it be outdoors?" Heather asked.

I shook my head. "I saw Steve setting up the firepits earlier today. Who doesn't love s'mores and hot cocoa?"

She nodded as she chewed on her lip.

"It's going to go great." I moved my hand out from the side of the box to squeeze her shoulder.

The box slipped out of my one remaining hand. Grace grasped it by its side. It twisted in her grasp, slipping between the smooth leather of her gloves, and plummeted toward the ground. We held our breath as the contents bounced around. Nothing fell out.

Heather started laughing first. Then we all joined in. I laughed, half wheezing, as a stitch formed in my side.

"Maybe I should carry that," Grace said as she kneeled to collect the box.

I bent over, winded. "That's probably a good idea."

For the last block, we fell into a companionable silence as we took in the sights. Over the past week, the decoration committee had been hard at work. Every winter, they covered the trees in downtown Point Pleasant with string lights, but now the trees were joined by rows of lights hung high above the streets. The lights clung to power polls and twined around business signs. They had turned the entire downtown into a winter wonderland. All it was missing was the snow. The warm air that came in off the Pacific Ocean kept the winters relatively mild in the Seattle region and even milder here on Whidbey Island. Tonight was the first time all the lights had been lit up. As we made the final turn toward the pier, my breath caught in my throat.

Rows of small campfires lined the beach. Every business had spruced up their signs. Even the Crab Shack had changed out its faded black-and-gray sign to something full color and bright; the orange of the cartoon crab almost glowed under the light of the full moon. The pier was bubbling with energy. It was almost like a photo from one of the walls of the Slice of Life Diner. Willow posted photos of the town, going all the way back to its founding. My favorite section showed Point Pleasant in the 1960s, when it was a thriving small town. The community had really outdone themselves.

"Oh, Heather…" Agnes choked, her voice thick.

"It came out okay." Heather blushed.

I swatted at her arm playfully. "Accept the compliment. This is amazing!"

Movement around the campfires drew us closer. Steve moved from fire to fire, directing the last of the setup. He wore a crisp tan suit with a red holiday-themed tie. His tight curls had been cut into a straight line across his forehead, the sides shaved into a precise fade. His smile widened as we approached.

"We are just setting up the last of the tables now," he said. "You can set up at the entrance."

We got to work. Boxes were unloaded. More decorations were hung. In the last thirty minutes, businesses arrived with items for their booths. The delectable scent of apple pie and fudge filled the air as Abby and Willow got to work at their food stations, each trying to outdo the other. They traded back and forth the coveted "Best Place to Eat Lunch" award from the Island County Gazette.

I stepped back from the table and shook glitter loose from my hands as I surveyed our work. The pier shimmered under the moonlight, lively and inviting. The warmth from the campfires and scattered propane heaters had left most of us with our jackets open and hats and scarves discarded. Grace still glowered. I suppressed a giggle. Her expression was at odds with the festive tinsel that had become caught in her hair while she worked.

"Let me help you with that." My fingers worked quickly to detangle the mess before the first guests arrived. I twisted the last piece out as Heather called me over to help hand out badges.

I lost track of faces as people poured in to attend the first-ever Point Pleasant Winter Intern Extravaganza kickoff party. All the students melded together. Almost every business along Marine View Drive had at least one assigned intern for the month.

I glanced up as the next group approached. The two boys couldn't have been more different. The one on the right towered over the crowd, his shoulders broad and his smile inviting. His chestnut hair hung over his forehead, looking almost windswept. The one on the left stood a full foot shorter and was wire thin. He fidgeted with his oversized coat. The smiling one spoke first.

"Sorry. I'm not actually on the list. I'm just tagging along with my roommate. Are plus ones allowed?"

"I don't see why not. We've got plenty of food." I reached for the blank stack of name cards. "What name should I put down?"

"Jay."

"Jay?" All of our name cards had last names.

He shuffled his feet. "Just Jay."

I wrote the letter *J* and handed it over. "And you are?" I asked his roommate.

"Ethan Sawyer."

I picked up his name tag and blinked. He was the only one interning off the main street. "You're interning with Victor, huh?" Victor was the local medical examiner.

"Yeah. I'm studying for my MCATs. I couldn't pass up an educational, paid opportunity." He scrunched up his face in concentration as he pinned his name tag to his jacket. "Unlike this guy, who gets to relax all break long."

Jay laughed. "Let me enjoy my last few months of freedom. I'll be joining the workforce here soon enough."

They wandered off into the crowd, and I lost track of them as I checked in the next few students. The groups slowed. Minutes passed between their arrivals until finally, the last name tag was claimed.

I stood to help Heather pack up when a woman approached the table. She wore a red peacoat, with her auburn hair loose around her shoulders. "Got space for one more?" she asked.

I pulled out one of the few remaining empty name tags. "I think so. Name?"

"Natasha."

"You a teacher, or...?" The first signs of crow's feet hugged the corners of her eyes. I placed her in her late thirties, a bit too old for most internship positions.

"Just visiting. It's a community event, isn't it?"

I nodded.

"They mentioned it when I checked in at my hotel. Has James Mitchell checked in?"

The name sounded familiar, but I had only lived in town for a few months. "I'm honestly not sure. I didn't help with that side of things."

"I think I saw his son come in earlier." She scanned the crowd. "Jay, or something like that."

I grabbed a pen to write her name, but the ink was out. I switched to a different one. We had been writing all evening, and they were all out.

"Oh, I've got one on me." She rifled through her bag and handed me a pen.

My hand clenched involuntarily around the pen as the muscles in my body tensed. The pen was heavy, as if it had been made of solid steel. I ran my finger along the engraving of her name on the side. I fought the urge to scan the crowd with her, as the sense of determined curiosity flowed through me from the pen.

How did Gran ever learn to deal with our psychometry ability? I refused to live in gloves like Grace.

The woman craned her head, looking past me as I jotted down her name.

"Here you go."

She snatched the name tag from me. I held up her pen, but she had already disappeared into the crowd.

"Strange lady," Heather commented.

"Yeah. Who's James Mitchell?" I asked, pocketing the pen.

"He's a real estate developer. He cosponsored this event."

"Never heard of him."

"Most of his projects aren't local. I mean, he has some stuff, but I think most of his portfolio is in other countries."

We chatted as we cleared the table. Over a hundred interns had filtered through, and with the added guests, there were at least three hundred people gathered along the board-walk and spilling out onto the pier. It was the busiest I had ever seen in it.

I left Heather at her hot cocoa station and wandered off to find Grace. She had disappeared early into the check-in process. I found her hovering near the Retirees. They were doing their best to ignore her gloomy presence by enter-taining a group of interns with town gossip. It wasn't anything I hadn't heard before. There was an outlandish rumor that Abby had broken into Slice of Life to steal Willow's key lime pie recipe. But there was also an opposing rumor that Willow had broken into Eats and Treats Bistro to steal Abby's triple-chocolate brownie recipe. The stories persisted, because everyone got a kick out of the mental image of them decked out in all black and doing ninja rolls through the kitchen. In truth, I doubted either woman wrote her recipes down. And they both had too much pride in their own work to steal someone else's. Betty had reached the part of the story where Abby allegedly escaped out the bathroom window with the recipe card between her teeth when the loudspeaker came to life a few feet away.

"If I could have everyone's attention, please." Steve's voice rang out over the group. Everyone turned toward the tempo-rary stage at the end of the pier, where he stood with a few local businessmen gathered around him. I only recognized half of them. "I wanted to take a moment to thank everyone for coming out and making the first annual Point Pleasant Winter Intern Extravaganza."

Grace sidled up next to Agnes while Steve continued his

presentation, welcoming the interns and thanking the local businesses for their participation. My gaze flicked between him and my daughter. She whispered into Agnes's ear, her expression animated. I inched in closer, trying to make out her words over the sound of the loudspeaker.

"If you can't help me, then at least teach me."

Agnes seized Grace by the hand and dragged her away from the group. I followed close behind. We huddled next to the Crab Shack, just outside the warmth of the heaters.

"Mel had a plan—"

"Gran isn't here. And I've read through all the notes we've found so far. I wasn't part of her plan. Don't I deserve to be part of someone's plan?"

I wrapped my arm around Grace's shoulders. "She's right."

Agnes sank against the wall. Defeated. "What did you have in mind?"

Grace's whole body shook. "Really, you'll help?"

Agnes nodded. "And I'll make Betty help, too, since she brought me into this mess."

Grace drew Agnes into a hug. "Thank you. Thank you. Thank you."

Agnes wiped a tear from the corner of her eye. "No need to thank me. We haven't started lessons yet."

"You're right. There's so much to study. This is going to be like... a witch's school for me. Give me homework. Tell me what to do. I want to learn."

Agnes chuckled. "A witch's school, huh?"

Grace nodded.

"And I suppose you'll also want lessons?" She eyed me.

I blinked and nodded. "I haven't been a student in a long time. But studying always seemed to go better in groups."

"All right. I'll talk to the girls, and we'll get a lesson planned."

"This week." Grace straightened.

"All right." Agnes held up her hands. "Now, can we get back to the party? I'm freezing over here. And these old bones don't bounce back as well as they used to."

We retreated from the wall and rejoined the party. Betty was deep in conversation with Ethan as we walked up. She was nodding and putting an arm on his shoulder. "Change is difficult."

"Did I miss something?" Agnes popped up at Ethan's elbow. Her ears must have been tingling. Gossip was the lifeblood of the Retirees.

"Oh, not much. Ethan's roommates with the Mitchell boy," Betty said.

"Oh? Well, that's going to be interesting for you." Agnes grinned.

Ethan cleared his throat. "Everyone has their first year out on their own. I can't imagine how he must feel going to a party sponsored by his dad after being cut off. I'm sure he'll be fine."

They continued chittering away, moving from topic to topic so fast, it was hard to keep up. I listened only partially paying attention. My mind was elsewhere. *A witches' school.* I wanted to learn about my heritage. I chewed on my lip. Badgering Agnes for lessons hadn't occurred to me. In hindsight, she had always been more willing to bend than Betty. That was probably why Gran hadn't put her in charge of watching over us. She'd known Betty would say no.

Grace stepped up next to me and handed me a hot chocolate. "When is this thing wrapping up?"

"I don't know."

"You want to get out of here? I'm tired."

We said our farewells, piled into the car, and headed home. Grace leaned her head against the window and closed her eyes. She wasn't sleeping. She hardly ever really slept anymore.

I patted her gloved hand. "I'm proud of you, honey."

She murmured something without opening her eyes.

We drove home in silence. She shuffled to her room and closed her door.

Charlie stood waiting for me at the top of the stairs.

"I'm sorry, buddy. I couldn't bring you with me today." I took the stairs up to my room.

He meowed back, objecting.

"If you had come with me, you would have been in the car all day," I explained as I emptied my pockets onto the nightstand. Natasha's pen clinked against the side of my alarm clock. "And Star was in the kitten room, so you wouldn't have had anyone to visit with at Heather's place."

He jumped onto the bed, circled, and turned his back on me.

"Oh, don't give me that." I crawled in after him and pulled him close. "You know I missed you."

He settled into my arms, purring. I scratched his chin.

A witches' school.

When I'd first found out Grace was a witch too, I was terrified. My transition wasn't as bad as I had expected, but it was scary. Hers was even scarier. Nightmares every night. I had trouble sleeping myself, knowing what she was going through. This was the first time in a long time that I'd felt at peace as I drifted off to sleep. We had hope again. We would get through this. Together.

CHAPTER 2

I stood up from my kneeling position in front of the bench and clapped my hands together. The winter chill had settled into my hands. *My hands?* I tried to look at them, but my head was already turning away as I walked down the pier. *Why am I here?* I couldn't get myself to stop. I kept walking. The boards of the pier creaked behind me. I turned toward the sound.

I stumbled, and pain radiated from where something heavy had hit me on the side of my head. *Not again. Not another death dream.* I lay on the ground, disoriented. But inside, I took in all the details. *I am on the pier.* The sky was lighter at the edges of the water. Dawn was coming. *I am on the pier before dawn.* Something—no, *someone* grabbed me by my ankle and yanked me backward.

My fingers dug into the wood. I looked forward blindly, staring at the Crab Shack. *What do my hands look like?* I screamed inside my head, but whoever's eyes I was staring out of, they weren't looking at their hands. They didn't look at anything that would identify when or who this was. *Pier before dawn. Crab Shack.*

Something touched my face.

My eyes opened, and I stared up at the ceiling of my bedroom. I lay twisted in the bedsheets and drenched in sweat. Charlie stood on my chest, staring at me, his paw raised above my face.

"Shoot." I beat my hands against the mattress. *Did I get enough? Will I be able to stop it this time?* Charlie stepped off me and sat on my nightstand. I jumped out of bed and looked out the window. It was dark, well before dawn. I fumbled with my phone, squinting against the bright light. It was 6:17 a.m. Dawn wasn't for another hour. *I still have time.* The words repeated in my mind as I threw on my clothes. Jumping from foot to foot, I shoved on one boot then the other. *I still have time.*

My car had frosted over in the night. I cursed under my breath as I cranked up the heat. Those words played through my head again and again as I scraped the ice from my windshield, my fingers numb from the cold. The minutes ticked by as I drove into Point Pleasant and through downtown. I pressed down on the accelerator as far as I dared. The roads wound in and out of the trees, my headlights bouncing off the eyes of nocturnal animals hiding in the brush.

I screeched to a stop in front of the pier twenty minutes later and froze. *What am I doing? I don't have a plan. What if the dream was about me? Can that happen? A self-fulfilling prophecy?*

I gritted my teeth and pushed open my car door. If it wasn't a self-fulfilling prophecy, then I couldn't risk staying in the car. I wasn't in my vision. My being here changed things. I crept down the pier, hugging my body against the buildings that stood on stilts above the water as I crept farther down the walkway. I gazed into the darkness, my eyes as wide as I could make them. The icy wind bit into my skin and stung my eyes. I blinked and continued to inch forward. The pier was deserted. The only sounds were the waves beating against the wooden beams and my own ragged breath.

I stalked from one end of the pier to the other. No one was there. I closed my eyes and replayed the dream. It wasn't dawn yet. *Am I too early?* In the dream, someone had grabbed my leg and dragged me. It was only a few seconds before Charlie woke me, but I saw the Crab Shack. *They pulled me away from the Crab Shack.* I retreated to that position and waited, crouching next to the old arcade building across the way.

No one came.

The sun rose behind me. I stood and paced again. *Was it not today? Then when?* I walked up and down the pier again, my eyes scanning every corner. My gaze traveled past the beach. I froze and looked back down. Lying in the sand was something dark and shaped like a person.

My heart leaped into my throat. I swallowed, trying to push it down. I ran for the stairs. I took them two at a time. My boots sank into the sand, and I jogged toward the form. As I got closer, I could make them out. It was a body. I sank to my knees. *How long have they been there? I thought I had time.*

My fingers were numb. I almost dropped my phone as I took it out of my pocket and dialed 9-1-1.

"9-1-1, what's your emergency?"

"I found a body." I struggled to get the words out.

The rest of the conversation passed in a blur as she asked where I was and if I knew who it was. I couldn't bring myself to turn them over. *I thought I had time.*

Chris arrived first, with Harrison in tow a few feet behind him. In the dim light, their tan deputy shirts seemed to float, as their dark pants blended into the ground behind them. Chris guided me back to the pier and sat me down next to a heater from the night before. He fiddled with it, turning it back on. The sudden heat shook me out of a stupor. I blinked up at him.

"What did you just say?" I asked.

"Did you see anyone else out here?" he asked.

I shook my head.

He crouched in front of me and held my hands between his. He rubbed them together and blew on them to help warm them up. "What were you doing out here, Dani?"

I had a nightmare. "I left something here last night and thought why not get it on my way to work?"

Heavy footfalls announced the sheriff's arrival. He had taken to wearing cowboy boots when the weather turned. Sheriff Robert Wright came to a stop over Chris's shoulder. His salt-and-pepper hair had grown in, brushing against the tops of his ears. He scowled at me. Ever since I figured out who killed Jessica, he had started to view me as a thorn in his side. "Why is it that whenever there's a body, I find you somewhere close by?"

Chris squeezed my hand as I mustered a weak smile. "Just lucky, I guess."

"I better not catch you meddling in this one." Bob huffed.

I opened my mouth to respond when Harrison called Bob over from under the pier. "We found an ID."

Bob turned on his heel and strode down the steps, barking orders.

A white van pulled up at the end of the pier, inching forward through a growing crowd of people. It came to a stop inches from the wooden beams, and Victor got out. He wore a heavy black duster with a Biltmore cap low on his head, covering his usual pompadour. His white beard had been recently trimmed, framing the sharp features of his face. His new winter intern, Ethan, scampered out of the van and ran around to the back to retrieve the gurney. He wore a too-large coat over pajama pants. While Ethan matched the crowd, Victor stood out. His strange mix of gothic Victorian was distinctive. The residents who lived over the shops downtown clustered in groups. They surged around the van. Victor calmly gestured for them to move back. He had a way of calming people. The anxious energy dissipated, and most of the crowd wandered back to their homes. Only a few lingered on.

Victor pulled out his pipe and lit it. He leaned against the van, small tendrils of smoke puffing out of his mouth. As he stood there, the color leached from his face. I leaned forward, my fingers gripping Chris's arm. Blood oozed down the side of Victor's face.

Not Victor. Please, not Victor. I blinked, and he was fine. The blood was gone.

"Are you sure you're all right?" Chris asked, his brow furrowed. "I can call someone if you need. I'm sure Heather's been up for at least an hour already."

I shook my head. "I'm fine."

I tracked Victor's movements as he clamped down onto the pipe, smothering the embers with the cap. His image flickered between now and... something else. Every time it flickered, the injuries were someplace else, like my vision was shifting through the possibilities. *Is this what an uncertain event looks like?*

"You don't look fine to me." Chris drew me in close and held me. He smelled of sandalwood and something else unique only to him.

I sank into his arms, and for a second, all thoughts of Victor left my mind. While we were still trying to figure out what we were to each other, I couldn't help but relax against him. In his arms was peace.

I peeked over his shoulder. Victor was disappearing down the steps. Ethan leaned sullenly against the van. My grip tightened around Chris as I followed Victor with my eyes while he strode down the beach. *When? What's going to happen? Please. Not Victor. Not someone I know.*

"I'm sorry, Dani. But I have to ask you more questions. Why don't we do this at the station? Being so close to where you found him must be hard."

"I..." I looked between Chris and Victor on the beach. *If*

he's here, surrounded by people, he should be okay. I nodded. "Okay. Let's go."

I followed Chris to his cruiser. We pushed our way past the few lingering onlookers. A woman in a red peacoat moved away from his vehicle as we made our way to his car, my mind still buzzing. I had been too late to save that man, but I would not be too late to save Victor.

"Who was he?" I asked when Chris settled in next to me.

He sighed. "Jim Mitchell."

I'd heard that name for the first time last night, and I'd never met him. *What good are these dreams if they are about strangers?*

CHAPTER 3

I followed Chris into the sheriff's station. Every time I came out here, the double-wide trailers looked more worn down around the edges. All the skirting was gone, leaving the cement blocks beneath clear to see. Weeds had grown up between the blocks, and a thick layer of moss clung to the gravel underneath. The floorboards creaked under our feet as he ushered me past Peggy at the front desk. She scrutinized me over her red-rimmed cat-eye glasses. I gave her a weak smile before Chris closed the door to the interview room, cutting her off from view.

"You need anything to drink? Water? Coffee?" he asked.

I shook my head. "Heather has me spoiled. I can't stand instant anymore."

He chuckled. "Me either. I think Harrison's the only one who touches the stuff. Harrison, or the poor souls who end up in the waiting room."

"So, what do you need to know?" I asked, shifting in my seat.

He sat down across from me and squeezed my hand. "I hate making you relive it again, but anything you remember could be helpful. Why don't you start at the beginning?"

"I woke up early. I don't know why, just had trouble sleeping, so I thought I would head into work early. When I was packing up my bag to head out, I realized I didn't have a pen Grace had given me. Last time I remember seeing it was at the check-in table at the kickoff party, so I thought I would swing by the pier to see if I could find it. I walked all over it but didn't see anything."

"Do you remember what time you got there?"

"Maybe six thirty? Six forty?"

"You searched for a pen for forty minutes?"

"It might have been a bit later than that. After I couldn't find it. It's been a while since I saw the sunrise over the water, so I thought I would sit out there for a bit. I got cold and started pacing a little. You know me. Too stubborn to go back in. And that's when I noticed a shape on the beach. A human shape. I thought it was a homeless man or something. Maybe someone from the kickoff party had too much to drink. But… it wasn't. When I got closer, he was too still." I choked on the last few words.

Chris squeezed my hand again. "You're doing great. Do you remember seeing any other cars or people when you arrived?"

"No. It was empty." *I thought I had time. How could I have been so wrong? Was it the sunset I saw? That can't be right. It was already dark when the party started. Someone would have noticed a body.*

"Do you remember seeing anything last night that stood out to you?"

"No. Was he there?" I wiped my eyes.

"He was a cosponsor. He was one of the guys up on the stage."

"Oh, right." I shook my head to clear it. *If it wasn't sunset, where did the light come from? A boat? Was there a witness?* "Heather mentioned that. I'd never heard of him before."

Chris had me go through everything a few more times

then sign off on my statement. "Thanks for that, Dani," he said as he stood. "Let me get this filed, and then I can get you back to your car."

I smiled. "Another ride in your cruiser, huh?"

He ran his hand through his hair and blushed. "What can I say? With the change in weather, we haven't had a chance to do our coffee dates in a while. Can you blame a guy for finding an excuse to get some time with you?"

I shook my head. "Are you still on Miller Farm duty?"

"For a few more weeks."

"Let's not let the weather stand in the way. I'll bring the coffee."

"And I'll bring the pastries." He grinned and backed out of the room.

I stood and peeked into the hall. At the historic location downtown, Chris would have had his own office. The county still hadn't repaired it after the massive plumbing leak that happened a few years before. In this cramped double-wide, he shared a desk with Harrison in what was designed to be a living room. He hummed as he worked. Peggy stiffened in her seat and glowered at him from her perch. Once upon a time, we had been friendly. But Peggy was loyal to a fault, and her loyalty was to the sheriff, who was not my biggest fan. Chris was still humming when the front door banged open. Chris's tune cut off as Bob strode into the room. Bob grabbed for the door before it could bang against the wall again. Outside, the wind gusted against the side of the building. He braced it as two men followed him inside. He carefully closed the door behind them.

The taller of the two I recognized, Jay from the kickoff party. His chestnut hair was disheveled and stuck out at odd angles from his head. His eyes were blurry and red rimmed. He wore an oversized sweater over pajama pants and tennis shoes. His shoulders hunched against the cold. The man next to him was a stark contrast. He stood upright, his

21

posture firm and poised. His salt-and-pepper hair was clipped close to his head, and even this early in the morning, it was well styled. Everything about him oozed money and prestige.

He glanced at his watch. "Will this take long?"

I inched closer to the ajar door and squinted down the hallway. *Who is he?*

"Not too long." Bob shuffled his feet, his ears reddening at the corners as he glanced around the lobby. It was worn around the edges. The plastic of the chairs in the waiting room was cracked, and the bulletin board across from them hung at an angle. The space hadn't been designed for long-term use, and it showed.

"Peggy, won't you be a dear and get Mr. Sterling a glass of water while he waits?" Bob asked.

She huffed and stood. She clattered around the kitchen, which was hidden from view by a black curtain hung from the ceiling.

Bob's ears became even redder as he combed his hand through his hair again. "Mr. Mitchell, this way, please."

Jay followed Bob into the hallway. Bob marched down the hall. His gaze flicked to me for a second as he passed, and he scowled. Jay didn't look up once. He shuffled, his feet barely leaving the ground, in a daze. I swallowed, pushing the rising emotions back down. I recognized that walk. It was how I'd moved for a week after I found out about Gran. Grief, for some people, was visible on the body.

At the end of the hall, the door to Bob's office opened and closed. I slipped out of the room and padded down the hallway. Peggy and Mr. Sterling sat in a stony silence. Peggy stiffened as I entered the room, but she stayed focused on her typing. I wandered closer to Mr. Sterling. I peeked at him out of the corner of my eye. The more I looked, the more familiar he became. I couldn't place where I knew him from, though.

"You must be Miss Williams," he said, his words clipped and cold.

Fighting the urge to flinch, I turned toward him, a smile plastered onto my face. "I am. And you are?"

"Bob warned me about you."

The smile froze on my face. *How do I respond to something like that?*

"He said you would probably come around asking questions." He sneered.

I shrugged, trying to keep a pleasant expression. "I've been known to be curious."

"I don't respond well to unwelcome curiosity." He stood and loomed over me. "Jim was a friend of mine. Questions should be left to the professionals."

I took a step back. He wasn't much taller than me, but something about the stiff way he stood, leaning inward toward me, made him seem larger. I had managed to push things aside during my conversation with Chris, but the images from my dream and vision I had of Victor still played in my head when I closed my eyes. I couldn't leave this alone.

Chris stepped up behind me and placed a hand on my shoulder. "You ready, Dani?"

I nodded and retreated from Mr. Sterling. He glowered at me and sat down. He perched stiffly on the edge of the plastic chair, his eyes tracking me as we left.

I followed Chris back to his cruiser and slipped into the passenger seat next to him. He reached across the seats and squeezed my hand. My heart fluttered at the contact.

"So what was that about?" he asked.

"I'm not sure. Bob apparently warned him about me, or something."

He barked out a laugh. "He's probably worried you're going to find the killer before him again."

I snorted. "It's only happened twice." *So far.*

We sat in silence for a few minutes as he drove. Normally,

23

our silences were companionable, but this time, there was a tense undercurrent. Chris kept both of his hands on the steering wheel, his shoulders hunched forward.

"Do you think you'll have time to get some breakfast with me?" I asked.

He relaxed in his seat. "Yeah."

I reached across the seat toward him, palm up. He dropped his hand into mine. We still hadn't been on an official full date. Things kept getting in the way. But in moments like this, it was clear we were inching our way into "more than friends" territory. I wound my fingers between his, and we drove, holding hands, into town. I stared out the window as we made our way through the backstreets toward the pier. The sky was blanketed by dark storm clouds that threatened rain. The trees along the roadway swayed in the wind.

"Looks like you're going to be busy soon," he said.

I nodded. Whenever a storm rolled through, my job as an independent claims adjuster became busy. I had been tracking the weather report. These clouds were just the beginning.

"Do you—"

My phone chimed in my bag, cutting him off.

I fished it out and checked my notifications. It was an email for a new claim. Chewing on my lip, I looked between my phone and the brewing storm. I didn't want to be out on the road when it really hit. "I think I'm going to need a rain check for breakfast."

He chuckled and squeezed my hand before letting it go to park the car. "I'm going to hold you to that."

Once the car came to a stop, he turned in his seat to look at me. I blushed under his gaze as comebacks floated through my head. Part of me wanted to say that the only way we could guarantee breakfast together was if he stayed the night, but we hadn't even kissed yet. There still a barrier between us. Years of marriage to his best friend from high school made things difficult. Being a witch made things more difficult. I bit my lip. He deserved someone who could be honest with him about everything.

"Where did you go?" He leaned forward, studying my face.

"What?" I blinked.

He held my gaze as he pushed a lock of hair behind my ear. "You got lost in thought for a second."

"I do that." I gestured out the window. "Just wondering how busy the weather is going to make me."

He sat back. "And here I was, hoping you were still thinking about breakfast."

I faltered. *I deserve happiness too. Isn't that why I stayed?* I squared my shoulders and held his gaze as I leaned toward him. "I was," I whispered into his ear as I drew him into a hug. I slipped out of the car before he could respond.

That was enough bravery for one day.

I scurried to my car, bent forward against the wind. It slipped in around the edges of my coat, chilling my neck and sending shivers down my spine. My teeth clattered together. I darted into my car and watched as Chris drove away in his cruiser. My chest constricted at the sight of him leaving. He had a calming presence. Every time we were together, I hoped we would get more time, but our responsibilities always pulled us in opposite directions. I got out my phone and read through the claims notification on my phone. It was for a tree limb down on a roof. It was much too windy to be clamoring around on roofs. The inspection would have to wait until the storm passed. I made a few quick calls from the car and headed toward home.

I came to a stop at an intersection and chewed on my lip as I stared up at the red light. The shorter way home was straight, but if I turned left, I could drive by Victor's. The shifting images of violence flitted through my head. *When?*

Who would want to hurt Victor? Maybe I need another look to make sense of it.

I flipped on my turn signal and inched out into the intersection when the light turned green. Gripping the steering wheel, I drove through town. I quickly left the small downtown area and wound my way into the residential neighborhoods that sprawled outward from the harbor. It was a small community, so the medical examiner's office did double duty as the local funeral home. It looked almost like a regular house from the outside. The only things that gave it away were the small sign in the front yard and the industrial style chimney in the back for the crematorium.

I slowed as I approached the building. The street was empty at this time of day. There were only a couple of cars parked along the road. By the amount of leaves and other debris littering their tops, they hadn't moved in a while. I rolled down the street, leaning forward against my steering wheel and straining to see any movement at the funeral home. The doors to the carriage house were open. I coasted to a stop and craned my neck to see inside. Victor's white panel van was parked inside, its back doors open. Ethan stood beside it, struggling to put away a hose. It was long and unwieldy in his hands. My eyes flicked between him and the main building. Victor was nowhere to be seen.

I closed my eyes and focused on my body. While my gran called it the Sight, it was more than that. I sometimes felt when things were off with my whole body, especially when I concentrated on it. I settled into my seat. My heart rate slowed. There were no prickles on my skin. No pressure behind my eyes. I shifted in my seat to a more comfortable position. There were no warning signs going off in my body. I opened my eyes and looked up at the house again. If something bad was going to happen to Victor, it wasn't happening now.

I glanced back at the carriage house. Ethan had detangled

the hose and was rolling it up into a neat bundle. He turned and saw me in the car. He jumped then smiled awkwardly, raising his hand in greeting. *Great. He's going to think I'm some sort of weirdo.* I waved back then grabbed my phone. Motioning to it, I pretended I had stopped to take a call.

He nodded, slammed the van door shut, and trudged back inside.

I sighed and leaned back in my seat. *If not now, when?* I would just have to make driving past the funeral home part of my routine. It wasn't like I could warn him about it. *What would I even say? "Hey, Victor, I had a prophetic vision"? Or... "I got this weird feeling"?* I shook my head and started the engine. *"Hey, Victor, have you received any death threats lately?" That would go over wonderfully. Not.*

The whole way home, my mind was on the dream and my visions. I drove through town on autopilot. Luckily for me, the streets were mostly empty, so the few times I did space out too long sitting at an intersection, no one was there to witness it.

I pulled into my driveway next to Grace's car. The second I exited the car, the chilly wind bit into my skin again. I hugged my coat to my body as I half ran, half stumbled my way to the house. The wind pushed into me, forcing me to clutch onto the banister as I climbed the steps to the front porch. I struggled against the screen door. It slammed behind me once I was inside, jerking my hand forward. The gas fireplace was on, casting a warm light around the tranquil room.

I found Grace in the kitchen. Charlie lay sprawled across the windowsill in front of her, his front paw stretched out to rest against her arm. His eyes were closed, and his tail twitched in his sleep. Grace sat on a stool, hunched over the counter, with both of my gran's journals open on either side of her.

My gran had left them to me as guides to explain how our magic worked. I only had the first two so far. I hadn't been able to find the last five. My gran had said they would come when I was ready. I always hated waiting for someone, or something else, to decide when I was ready, especially when it wasn't just about me. Grace needed help more than I did. Even inside the house, she wore gloves to prevent her from picking up any lingering emotional residue.

"What are you working on?" I asked as I filled the kettle and put it on the stove.

"A study plan." She tapped one of the two journals. "I always end up with more questions than answers. I've been writing them down. Since Agnes agreed to teach me, I'm organizing them into categories."

I peered over her shoulder. She was shuffling around stacks of Post-it Notes covered with questions. She picked up a stack and began breaking it down into three groups.

"I figured I should be able to ask three to four questions a session, with some time for follow-ups." She held up one of the sticky notes and read it off to me. "Is it possible to look back further than a week? If so, how far back, and do you know how to modify the memory recall spell to do so?"

I rocked back on my heels. She had easily a hundred sticky notes with questions on them. "Are they all so detailed?" I asked.

She shrugged. "It's a question worth asking."

"It seems a bit... ambitious."

She tensed. "What's that supposed to mean?"

"I'm just worried that you're biting off more than you can chew." I grimaced as the words left my mouth. *And here I am, acting like Gran.*

She spun on the stool and glared at me. "More than I can chew? You've had months more to practice than I have. Months. If I don't get a handle on this, I might never get a good night's sleep again. Shouldn't you be more concerned about my lack of sleep than a study schedule?"

I took a step back and held up my hands. "You're right. I just—"

"Just what?" she spat.

"Don't want you getting your hopes up. They don't have the Sight."

"They're witches, aren't they?"

"Yes."

"Who understand how magic works?"

I sighed. "Yes."

"Then that's all I need from them. An explanation. And I'll figure the rest out on my own." Grace spun back to her sticky notes and roughly collected the piles.

"Honey..." My hand hovered over her shoulder. "I'm here."

"Are you going to tell me about the dream you had?" She didn't look at me as she continued sorting her notes.

"How'd you know?" I sagged against the counter next to her.

"I heard you." She peered at me out of the corner of her eye, a subtle smile on her lips. "I don't sleep much, remember?"

I rubbed the bridge of my nose. "It was about a murder. I didn't wake up in time to stop it."

"I'm sorry." She reached out and squeezed my hand.

"Me too. A study schedule is a great idea. It's just... everything is so overwhelming. It scares me sometimes, you know?"

She nodded. "I was thinking about running it by the Retirees." She flipped through her sticky notes. "Maybe they should sort the questions instead of me."

"That sounds like a great idea." I drew her into a tight hug, tucking her head under my chin. "And once you've got the first session scheduled, let me know so I can clear my schedule for it."

Grace hugged me back. "Sorry about getting mad at you."

I rubbed her back. "It's okay. Neither of us has been sleeping well."

"But we will be soon, right?" She pulled away from me and wiped a tear from her cheek. "Because this witch school idea is going to work."

"I hope so." I moved to the oven and took the kettle off the burner. "Tea?"

"I would love some."

I made us each a steaming cup of Earl Gray and settled into the stool next to Grace. "Why don't you show me all the questions you have so far?"

She perked up and began sorting through the piles again. She really had over a hundred questions. And almost all of them were about our family's curse.

CHAPTER 4

After spending a few hours going over all of Grace's questions, I ended up tossing and turning all night. Whenever I drifted off to sleep, I was back at the pier, clawing at the deck planks as someone pulled me toward the steps from behind. And when that wasn't playing through my head, it was Victor. He walked toward me, blood dripping from his head or his chest. Every few seconds, the injury shifted to another part of his body. He had been so kind to me after my grandfather George had died, and even kinder after Gran. While he was a little eccentric, I had never met someone so skilled at walking with someone through the grieving process. He had a gift.

I glanced over at my nightstand. It was still cluttered with the miscellaneous items I had picked up at the kickoff party. I lifted myself onto my elbows to read the time. It was just before six. Groaning, I dropped back onto my pillow. I had gotten maybe two hours of sleep all night, but rolling back over now would be pointless. I climbed out of bed and padded toward the bathroom to get ready for the day. Charlie yawned, stretched, and followed me, his eyes groggy from sleep.

"You up for coming into the office with me today?"

He yawned again and rubbed against my legs, purring.

"You know you're probably going to get wet? It's going to be raining most of the day."

He sat back on his haunches and stared up at me, his blue eyes pondering. He cocked his head to one side, stood, then rubbed himself against my legs again before jumping up onto the counter to watch me.

"I'll take that as a yes." I chuckled and picked up my toothbrush.

I chattered at him about my plans for the day as I went through my morning routine. He watched me the whole time, adding the occasional meow as if agreeing with me when I asked a rhetorical question. Once my morning routine was done, he followed me out into the hall and down the stairs. He waited patiently for me to affix his harness, then he jumped into my arms before I headed out for the day. I chuckled. Normally, he walked, but today, he wanted to be carried so his paws wouldn't get muddy.

Charlie sprawled across the passenger seat next to me as I drove into town. He chirped at me when we got to the intersection that would either take me downtown or go farther into the residential areas. I reached over and scratched him under his chin. He leaned into my hand, purring. I inched the car forward and peered into the intersection. Rainwater made the roadway slick, making the asphalt dark and the lines difficult to see. Charlie stood up in his seat and squinted out the window at the houses.

"Yeah. I'm going to check on Victor."

He swished his tail, and we continued driving on in silence.

There was a tenseness in his body, and in mine, as well. I gripped the steering wheel as we got closer. I turned onto Victor's street. Red and blue lights flashed outside his home.

A gasp escaped my lips as my heart leaped into my throat. My hands trembled as I drove closer. *Please be okay. Please be okay.*

I came to a stop across the street. There was no one outside, but his front door stood partly ajar. I fumbled with my seat belt.

"Stay here," I whispered to Charlie as I bolted out of the car. My legs shook under me as I crossed the street and took the wooden steps of his porch two at a time. Rainwater soaked my hair and slipped down my back. *Please be okay.*

I pushed open the door to the funeral home and froze.

Bob turned toward me and scowled. "What are you doing here?" he barked.

My gaze traveled past him to Victor. He stood between Bob and Harrison. His normal regency wear was covered in a lab coat.

I slumped against the doorjamb and exhaled sharply. "You're okay."

"I'm mortified. I've been in this business for well over thirty years, and not once have I lost a body before." Victor wrung a pair of surgical gloves with his hands. As he shifted under the light, he changed.

My jaw dropped, and my eyes went wide as his image shifted from one injury to another, sometimes with less than a second between them. *What is going on?* It was as if the future couldn't decide on how he was going to be killed, only that it was going to happen.

Bob moved between us. He rocked forward on his toes to loom over me. He jutted his chin forward and stared down his nose at me. "Ms. Williams, your presence is not needed, nor was it requested, at this potential crime scene." He emphasized the words *crime scene*. "Leave, before you cause more of a disruption."

I swallowed and backed out of the door. I peeked over his

shoulder at Victor one last time before Bob slammed the door in my face. My last image of Victor was of dead eyes.

I trudged back to my car in a daze, my clothes already soaked. There was no use in running. I climbed into the car and sat there picking at my cuticles. Charlie hopped up onto the dashboard and perched above the steering wheel. He watched me with his bright-blue eyes. After a minute, he chirped in question.

"I think someone is going to kill Victor," I murmured. "But I don't know when, or where. Or why. Why would anyone want to hurt him?"

Charlie inched forward and let out another meow. I reached out and rubbed my thumb between his ears. I didn't know how I knew, but I did. Charlie was telling me to investigate.

"Thanks, buddy."

I turned on the engine. In the beam of light from my headlights sat another car. The car hadn't been there when I'd arrived. I drove past it slowly. Seated in the front seat was a woman. Her chestnut hair was pulled into a high ponytail, and she was wrapped up in a red peacoat with a long black-and-gray scarf piled high around her neck. *The woman from the pier?*

Our eyes met. She froze. She awkwardly raised her phone and motioned to her ears.

I narrowed my eyes. My mind went back to the day before, when I had pretended to be on the phone to avoid an awkward conversation with Ethan. *Is she doing the same thing? It's an odd hour to be taking calls.* I studied her face, etching it into my memory, then continued forward. I had claim files to set up at work.

I spent a few hours setting up files and completing reports for my clients. It wasn't long before I heard Olivia, my office neighbor, arrive across the foyer. I had a roof to inspect before the weather turned, so I packed up my stuff and popped over to her office before heading out.

Olivia hummed as she moved around her office. I knocked on the doorjamb, and she craned her neck around to see me. She wore a striking burnt-orange sweater dress with her hair in twists around her face. Her face broke into a wide smile as Charlie trotted into her office next to me.

"You mind watching the little guy while I'm out?" I asked.

She crouched down to pet him. "I could never refuse the office mascot. Although I'm not sure if 'little guy' is accurate anymore."

I barked out a laugh. "I wish you could convince him of that. He's still convinced he's as small as when I got him and jumps up on me like he still weighs less than a pound."

When I had first gotten Charlie, he could fit into the palm of my hand. Now he was almost ten pounds. He looked like a fully grown cat, but he wasn't even six months old yet. Over the past few months, he had developed giant paws that he hadn't fully grown into. I had a feeling he was going to be a ginormous cat once he finished growing. If it wasn't for his coloration, almost fully white with some caramel colors around his ears, I would have thought he was part bobcat. He looked like a stereotypical ragdoll, only much bigger.

I bid her farewell and backed out of the office. I threw on my Williams Adjusting hoodie and plucked my still-damp coat from the back of my chair to put on over it once I was outside. The wind was due to pick back up in the afternoon, and I wanted to get as much of my exterior inspections done before the weather turned. I packed up my gear and grabbed my thermos. It was almost empty. I looked over at my coffee maker. It was never as good as Heather's. A quick stop wouldn't add too much time to my morning.

I walked over to the Bizzy Bean. Star, Heather's cat, peered at me from inside the enclosed cat space inside the café. Kittens zoomed around the room behind her. She looked around at my feet and, not seeing Charlie, turned away and sauntered back to her cat tower. I chuckled and walked up to the counter to order a drink.

Heather took my order. "How's your morning so far?"

I shrugged. "It's been a weird day."

She came around the counter and guided me to our usual spot in the back. One of the new foster kittens joined us at the table. It scampered around under our feet and playfully swatted at the edges of my coat that hung over the side of the bench. Heather pushed my coffee into my hands. "Tell me about it."

"I think the body I found yesterday may have gone missing."

"Wait, what? What body?" She inched forward in her seat.

"Oh, I thought…" I flapped my hands, lost for words. "I guess I thought because news travels fast around here that you would have heard. I found Jim Mitchell's body at the pier."

She sat back in her seat and crossed her arms over her chest. "And how exactly do you know it's gone missing?"

I winced. "I drove past Victor's this morning."

She tapped her foot. "You're investigating again, aren't you?"

I hung my head. I didn't know how to respond to that. Heather knew me better than most. I couldn't hide my curiosity from her. But I also couldn't explain it either. "Maybe a little?"

She reached out and gripped my hands. She held them as she studied my face. "Dani, after the last time? The last two times? Are you sure it's safe?"

"I—"

"You know you don't have to investigate every death that

happens in town, right? I mean, Bob isn't the greatest sheriff, but Chris is a good deputy. Don't you trust him to find the right guy?"

I shifted in my seat. I did trust Chris. But I'd seen Victor hurt for a reason. *What if Chris can't keep Victor safe?* I chewed on my lip.

"And I don't know Grace well yet. Mostly because she's about as closed off to new people as a teenager can get. But she seems like she's still struggling with something. She needs you."

"I know—"

"I need you." Heather gave my hands one last squeeze. "And now that is out of the way. Who do you think did it?"

I blinked. "You're sending mixed signals."

She laughed. "As much as I would like to think you'd listen to my sound advice, your curiosity wouldn't let you. And my curiosity won't let me not try to get the latest update."

My whole body shook as I tried to hold in the laughter. I wiped a tear from the corner of my eye. "Honestly, I don't know. I didn't know the man."

Heather inched forward in her seat and leaned against the table. "So what's the first step, then?" she whispered with a conspiratorial grin on her face.

"Statistically, it's usually someone you know. So… make a list of associates?"

Heather began ticking people off. "There's his son, Jay. His business partner, Alex. I think they had a staff of about twenty. So at least all those employees. I think he's divorced, so his ex-wife. Is she still in town?"

Shrugging, I pulled out a notebook and jotted down the names she mentioned. I glanced up as the front door opened. The Retirees entered, all clad in matching red-and-green-striped hooded tracksuits. Faux fur from the hoods poked out from behind their shoulders. I motioned them over. They exchanged a look then shuffled toward our table en masse. They spoke over each other, each one giving a different variation of good morning.

I bit back a grin. "We were just wondering if you had heard anything interesting about Jay Mitchell."

They exchanged another look. Betty took a step forward. "So you're investigating again, are you?"

She melted back as Sarah stepped into her place. "If you're looking into Jay, you're probably looking in the wrong direction."

Agnes batted her away. "I think she means if you're looking at him for a financial motive. He didn't have it. The Mitchells are a strange bunch."

Betty wrapped her arm around Agnes and tugged her back so Sarah could inch forward again.

"As I was saying." Sarah shot Agnes a glare. "He wouldn't inherit anything if his dear old dad passed away."

"Why's that?" I asked.

"Because of the Mitchell tradition." Sarah straightened.

Agnes poked her head over Sarah's shoulder. "For the past few generations, at least, they've had a tradition of leaving their estates to charity. Once they've set up the trust fund, nothing else gets added."

"I think it started with James Mitchell, the first," Betty added. "He thought inheriting everything led to weakness."

"Oh? I thought it started with his brother, Harold?"

They started bickering over which Mitchell brother had started the tradition, but they were all convinced that Jay would inherit nothing from his dad outside of his trust fund.

"Which charity did Jim pick?" I asked.

Sarah turned to me, her gray eyes striking against her mostly black hair. "Haven of Hope in Oak Harbor."

They wandered off, still in a deep debate over the town's history. I slumped into the booth. "When I saw Jay at the sheriff's station, he looked heartbroken. If he didn't have a financial motive, maybe he shouldn't be on the list?"

"You saw him?"

I filled her in on my visit to the station.

"That's odd," she commented when I was done.

"What's odd?"

"Alex Sterling." She glanced over at the Retirees to make sure they weren't listening in. They had moved on from that topic and were now discussing what to serve at the winter intern close-out bash they were in charge of. "You've got a good track record of ferreting stuff out. If he doesn't want you involved, it could mean he's hiding something."

I nodded. "I thought about that. But I don't know how Bob characterized my past involvement. I doubt he was complimentary."

"If he was hiding something, I bet one of their employees would know. Workers always know when there's tension in the office."

"That's a great idea." I pushed myself up, but she grabbed my arm when I was half out of the seat.

"Dani…" She fumbled for her words. "Can you promise me something?"

"Of course." I put my hand over hers. "Anything."

"If you're going to do something dangerous, make sure you have backup. I… I don't want to think about what could have happened if I wasn't there when you had your show-down with Brad. He pulled a gun on you. He could have killed you."

I swallowed. Her calling the cops when she saw things get tense had saved my life. He was much larger than me. But I also didn't know when I might need to cast some spells, and it wasn't like I could have anyone other than the Retirees or Grace around for that. *Stop it. She's worried. Stop justifying things to yourself.*

"Okay."

"Oh, and you have to keep me updated, so I know when you need help. Tell me the minute you find something new. And to not charge off on your own or to do a stakeout without adequate supplies."

"I will."

"You have to promise."

I chuckled. "Okay. I promise."

CHAPTER 5

While I was in the Bizzy Bean, I received two more claim notices on my phone. It was going to be a very busy week. The first was for more downed tree limbs, and the second was for vandalism damages. I confirmed receipt of both and called the claimants to set up inspections. The wind was already picking back up, so I scheduled the downed tree limb for later in the week and headed out to look at the vandalism damages.

The claim took me into one of the oldest parts of Point Pleasant. As I moved along the water's edge, the houses grew farther and farther apart, with large sprawling lawns and well-maintained hedges lining the roadways, blocking most of the houses from view. As I drove into the neighborhood, the cars shifted to Mercedes Benzes and BMWs with the occasional large Ford truck devoid of any dirt or signs of wear thrown into the mix. I came to a stop across the street from a neighborhood playground and parked behind a locksmith's black van.

When I stepped out of my car, raised voices greeted me. I glanced at my watch. I was a few minutes early for my appointment. It was hard to make out what they were saying over the rushing wind and the banging coming from the home I was there to inspect. My curiosity piqued, I leaned against my car and muttered the words to the spell to heighten my senses. Motes of light fluttered around me, settling into my skin. I kept my eyes closed against the sudden brightness of the day. I focused, dampening one sense after the other, until only my hearing was improved.

Even with the improved hearing, I couldn't make out the words. Not entirely. Every word was interrupted by a hammer fall. I sighed and dropped the spell. I followed the raised voices the old-fashioned way. Two doors down, I found Jay gesticulating wildly over a woman who barely came up to his chest. Her golden-blond hair streaked with white was piled on top of her head in a messy bun. She wore dirt-encrusted pants with an olive-green jacket over the top. She held a gardening hoe in one hand and thrust a bony finger into his face with the other.

"I did not stand for it from your father, and I will not stand for it from you either," she said, stomping her foot.

Jay saw me over her shoulder and blanched. "I don't have time for this right now," he said. "Why don't you come back with your lawyer?"

The woman threw her hands up and spun around toward me. She glowered at me and stalked past me to the house next door, muttering under her breath. I stared after her as she slammed the front door.

Jay shifted uncomfortably under my gaze. He ran his hand through his hair and slouched as he stepped down off his porch. "You're that lady from the police station yesterday, aren't you?"

I nodded and stepped toward him, hand outstretched. "Dani Williams. I'm with Williams Adjusting. There was a break-in next door I'm here to look at."

His hand was warm and his handshake firm. I held his

gaze. His eyes were still red rimmed, and his nose was raw and puffy.

A cold or was he crying?

"I'm Jay."

"You okay? That looked a little intense."

He snorted. "Gladys Palmer. It's a long story."

"I've got time." I forced a weak smile onto my face.

He looked back at the house and shuffled his feet.

"I think we met briefly at the kickoff party. You were a plus one, weren't you? I helped out at the check-in table," I said, cutting into his thoughts.

"Right." He tried to smile, but it didn't sit right on his face. "Ethan's hopeless at being social."

"You must be good friends."

He shrugged. "I guess. I haven't known him for long. We got assigned to the same dorm, and both needed a place when our roommates bailed on us. He's a good guy, though. He lost his dad, too, so he knows what I'm going through. It's been really helpful having him around."

"Was he there when you… found out?" I asked.

Jay collapsed into himself, hugging his arms to his body. "Yeah. We had hung out together most of the night. When I woke up to him banging on my door, I thought… I don't know what I thought. That he needed a ride or something? First-day jitters." He looked up at the sky, blinking rapidly to keep the tears at bay. "God, what am I going to tell my mom?"

He shook himself and looked back at the house.

"I'm so sorry for your loss."

Jay nodded and took a step back. "I've got to get back in there. Got a lot of stuff to do. A funeral to plan for."

I studied his back as he retreated up the steps. His grief was palpable and real. I mentally checked Jay off the list. My first read of him felt right. He couldn't have done it. Once the front door closed, I followed my footsteps back to my car and got my camera for my inspection.

I followed the sound of hammering to the backyard. A petite woman, no more than five feet tall, hovered over a construction worker who was boarding up the window next to her back door. Her silver hair was cut into a smart bob. She wore an oversized sweater, which she hugged to her small frame as she hopped around, pointing out other issues at the back door.

I came to a stop at the bottom of the stairs leading up to the back door. "Ms. Mabel Henderson?"

She spun in place, her face breaking out into a wide smile. Her green eyes sparkled as she descended the stairs, two at a time. "You must be Ms. Williams. The adjuster?"

I nodded and shook her hand. "That I am. I understand there was a break-in?"

She nodded, her face solemn. She turned back toward the stairs and guided me up them. "They broke in back here. I took photos of the window before he started boarding it up. It's such a pity about that window, though. Stained glass. I'm not sure if the artist is still alive. I got it when I was a teenager." She continued on, explaining the window's origin and emotional value and how beautiful the doves were in the spring when the light would hit them just so. I smiled and nodded through the explanation and took photos of all the other areas she pointed out as being damaged. Fortunately, just inside the door, there were hardwood floors, so the glass had been easy to clean up. "Anyway, it doesn't look like they went past here."

I peered over her shoulder into the living room area. It was filled with antique furniture. Over the mantelpiece, there were crystal candleholders and a large TV. "Have you noticed anything missing?"

She nodded, wringing her hands. "All they took were my keys. Do you think they are coming back? My grandson said

I should get myself a dog. But I don't know about all that. Rekeying the house should be enough, right?"

"I don't know. Maybe your grandson could stay with you for a few days?"

"He's on a fishing boat on the coast of Maine. I'm surprised I caught him at all. I was lucky enough to snag a call spot first thing this morning."

I imagined my gran staying in her home alone after a break-in. I bit back a grin. A thief wouldn't have expected a witch to greet them, but I doubted Mabel was a witch. "Well, if you're worried, you could always foster a dog for a little while."

"That's a brilliant idea. I'll foster." A mischievous grin settled over her face. "Oh, the ladies at the club will be tripping over themselves trying to one-up a foster situation. Philanthropy is like a competitive sport to those ladies. Do you think they have any three-legged dogs or ones missing an eye available? They couldn't outdo me then."

I chuckled. "Couldn't hurt to ask. Now, is there any damage inside?"

She walked me through the damages again. It was all to the window. I snapped a few more photos, asked her to send me a list of the keys, and headed out.

I stood on the sidewalk and glanced around to see if there were any houses that had a clear view of the back door. There weren't. Each property was lined with trees or tall privacy fences. My gaze stopped at the house Gladys Palmer had disappeared into.

There was almost a clear view. And her conversation with Jay had been intense. *Two birds with one stone?* Smiling, I made my way up her walkway and knocked on her front door. She didn't answer. I pulled out a business card and slipped it into her screen door with a note.

I am investigating a break-in across the street and wanted

to know if you have seen anything unusual in the neighbor-
hood. Please call me if you've seen anything.

If Mabel was like any of her neighbors, they liked to gossip. The Retirees would fit in nicely here. They could definitely give Mabel a run for her money. Still smiling, I made my way back to my car.

CHAPTER 6

The entire drive back to the office, I replayed the interaction with Jay and Gladys in my head. Jay had mentioned a lawyer. *Was there some sort of legal dispute? The judicial system moves slowly. Maybe Gladys got impatient?*

I didn't know much about Jim Mitchell, so it was hard to know what was or wasn't important. If he was a public figure, finding out stuff about him wouldn't be too difficult. I parked in front of my building and strode into my office.

Charlie scampered out of Olivia's office and followed me across the foyer into mine. He twined himself between my legs as I sat down and got to work. While my photos downloaded from my camera, I dug into Jim Mitchell. I started on his obituary, noting down the other names mentioned, then moved onto his social media profiles and his business website. Every time I encountered a new name, I jotted it down and noted the connection. The list grew quickly. He was well connected in the community. And there were no signs of any bad press. Even the bad reviews of his business online were about his business partner, not him. I chewed on my lip as I dug farther. I opened the Island County Court website. The only record of a court case was a divorce, which happened fifteen years before. I noted her name, too, and went back to his social media profiles. They were best friends. He walked her down the aisle when she got remarried last year.

I sat back in my chair and groaned. Charlie jumped into my lap and headbutted my chin. He purred as he curled up to make biscuits in my lap. Jim Mitchell's public persona was squeaky clean. Maybe his being a public figure made things worse. It was obvious he had someone who helped him curate his public image. *An employee, maybe?*

I stroked Charlie's fur as I went back to the company's website and reread all the names and job titles. I paused over Emily Thompson, online communities director. *Is that a fancy name for a social media manager?*

I clicked on her picture and read through her company biography. It was another name for a social media manager. I poured through her online profiles. As I scrolled past the third week of posts, I noticed something. Every Wednesday, she had a check-in at Abby's bistro for lunch. I leaned forward in my chair as I flipped between all the Eats and Treats Bistro check-ins. Every Wednesday for almost a year. I grinned.

As if sensing the change in mood, Charlie jumped off my lap and darted toward the foyer. I grabbed my coat and followed him out into the foyer. He led me to the front door, rubbed against my legs one last time, then sauntered off to Olivia's office.

I chuckled. "It was nice to see you, too, buddy."

I slipped out the front door, hugging my jacket to me, and jogged the couple blocks to Abby's.

I smelled her place before I saw it. She had a habit of leaving her front door open, even this time of year, so the scents of her cooking would waft out into the street to entice more people inside. My stomach grumbled as I approached. In the winter months, Abby's menu shifted from light and citrusy to filling and full of nostalgia. It was the season for chilis and stews. I inhaled deeply as I stepped into the bistro. The space heater hanging from the ceiling instantly warmed me as I entered the building. The space was decorated with a mix of retro-fifties vibes and industrial. Steel tables were scattered around the room over a red enamel floor. She had added a jukebox to the back corner. It played a strange mix of Elvis, ABBA, and Simon and Garfunkel. Somehow, it worked. I shrugged off my jacket and followed my nose to the counter that ran along the far wall, my mouth watering at the scent of chicken and dumplings.

Abby wore an ugly Christmas sweater over black slacks, her honey-brown hair pulled back into a low ponytail. She smiled at me as I approached. "I don't normally see you in on Wednesdays."

"I smelled the chicken from outside. I couldn't resist."

"It's been real popular today. The carrot cake has been a close second. They go pretty well together. You want a slice of that, as well? If so, you should probably snag a piece now before it's all gone." She cocked her head over to the conveyor belt for desserts that ran the length of the counter. A group of interns sat perched in front of it, a stack of mini plates surrounding them.

I chuckled. "You know me too well. Could I get a second piece? Both of them to go? Olivia loves your frosting."

Abby nodded and boxed up everything.

After I got my food, I retreated to a table in the back and watched the front door. Emily was nowhere to be seen, but if her posting history revealed anything, she was a creature of habit, and any minute now, she would walk through those doors. I was halfway through my soup when she entered. I almost missed her; she had such an unassuming presence. Her mousy brown hair was frizzy. The light of the space heater bounced off the flyaway hairs, giving her a haloed effect before she shuffled farther into the building. She was tiny, with an oversized sweater pulled down over her hands. She wore leggings and simple black boots. I wolfed down the rest of my soup while she ordered.

Emily sipped on apple cider as she waited. I stared at her drink, leaning forward in my seat, and murmured the words to the relaxation spell. Motes of light drifted from my mouth and swirled around the room, invisible to everyone but me. They settled over her drink as she took another sip. I held my breath, waiting for the spell to take hold. After a few seconds, the warm glow from her drink settled onto her skin. I snatched my pre-bagged desserts from the table and made my way toward her.

She stood there, with her head bowed over her phone, tapping away. She didn't look up as I approached. I chewed on my lip. The relaxation spell always helped. It made people feel trusting, so they were more likely to spill their secrets. But it affected everyone differently. Secretive people were still secretive, and it took a few well-placed questions to get them to open up. I ran through what I knew of her in my head. She handled their social media but also wore another hat as a community outreach coordinator. I suspected she was the one who organized most of the Mitchells' involve-ment in the winter internship program.

I plastered a smile on my face and stepped into her field of vision. "Emily! It's so nice to see you again."

She looked up and blinked. Her eyes were wide behind her thick-rimmed glasses. They had a funky Christmas design with little snowmen dancing on the arms.

"Sorry. I don't know if we were ever formally intro-duced," I said, holding out my hand. "I've been helping Heather out with the winter internship events. I tagged along to a few of the meetings."

She tucked her phone in her pocket. "Oh right, of course. I think I remember seeing you there."

Success. I loved it when my gambles paid off. I shifted to a somber stance. "Honestly, I'm surprised to see you out and about. Does Alex still have you working, despite what happened? I would have thought the office would have shut down for at least a few days."

Her eyes glistened as she shook her head. "Business never sleeps."

"How are you holding up?"

"About as well as expected. I've been working on the company announcement all day. Not all our partners know yet."

"I just can't believe it. He always seemed so nice. Who would even want to hurt him?"

She pursed her lips and looked to the side.

I lowered my voice and inched in closer. "Do you know something?"

"I really shouldn't—"

The glow of the spell was fading. I gritted my teeth as I nodded. She had stopped sipping on her drink, so this was probably my last chance to ask a question while her guard was down. "I understand. I wouldn't want to upset Alex either."

"It's not that." She looked around and dropped her voice to match mine. She whispered to me, a conspiratorial gleam in her eye. "I had to go into his email accounts after he passed. I had no idea, but for the past three months, he had been chatting with a woman. It was getting a little spicy, if you know what I mean. He sent her gifts. Expensive gifts. After the last one, he asked to meet in person. I got the impression it was going to happen soon. What if he was being catfished, and things went south when he found out? He was a good guy. But I know a lot of people just saw dollar signs when he was involved."

"Wow. That's..." *Unexpected.* I blinked. "Who was she? Do you know?"

"I don't know. But she went by the username Twist-edTales."

Before the spell ended, I pushed one last time and managed to get the name of the site Jim had met the mystery woman on, as well as her email address. As the last of the light faded, I stepped back, smiled again, and gave Emily my condolences before I scurried back to the office.

Charlie met me at the door. I followed him into Olivia's office, holding the bag from the Bistro behind my back. Olivia was on the phone when I came in. She smiled at me in greeting and continued talking to one of her clients. I tuned her out as I made my way to the back room to get plates. As I heated the caramel sauce in the microwave, I fiddled with my phone. It had been a while since I used the incognito function on my web browser, but the last time I looked up something random like "cat socks," I had advertisements for weeks about them. While cat socks were cute, I didn't want advertisements for dating services.

I went to the site Emily had mentioned and searched for TwistedTales. I found her profile quickly enough, but I couldn't see anything without downloading the app and creating an account. Cursing under my breath, I made a quick throwaway account with an old email address I didn't use anymore.

There weren't any photos of her face. It was odd, but every photo was atmospheric and set a mood. She remained a mystery. I read through her About Me section and chuckled.

In a world full of long walks on the beach, I'm more of a dance-in-the-rain kind of person. Connoisseur of the mysterious and the marvelous, I navigate life with a dash of curiosity and a sprinkle of whimsy. You won't find my face plastered all over this profile—I prefer to keep a bit of mystique, like a book waiting to be opened. I can promise you an adventure. Lover of deep conversations and spontaneous escapades, I'm on the lookout for someone who can keep up with a rapid-fire exchange of banter, appreciate the beauty in the ordinary, and believe that genuine connection goes beyond a profile picture. If that sounds like you, then you might just be the missing piece to my puzzle. Let's make our own story, one filled with laughter, late-night conversations, and a touch of the unexpected.

It was playful and fun. I could understand why someone would message her. I hovered over the Contact Me button. It showed that she was online. *What would I even say? "Hey, did you catfish and murder Jim?"* The microwave beeped next to me. I jumped, almost dropping my phone. I picked up the caramel and poured it over the cream cheese frosting on the carrot cake. My mouth watered at the scent.

"What have you got in there?" Olivia called from the other room.

"A surprise!" I yelled back.

I stared at the Contact Me button on my phone for a few more seconds.

Charlie bumped against my leg, purring.

"You trying to encourage me, buddy?" I asked.

He chirped in response. I exhaled and pressed the button. I sent a quick message.

DANI:
I think we have a friend in common.

Within seconds, TwistedTales had read the message. I stared at the little photo of a sunset, waiting. A few seconds later, she was offline. I shoved my phone into my pocket, grabbed the carrot cakes, and walked out.

"It's an Abby special. It seemed like a crime to eat it on my own."

Olivia squealed with delight as I handed her the plate and dug in. "You spoil me," she said after her first bite.

We settled in and chatted over the cakes.

CHAPTER 7

The rest of the day went by slowly. I spent the afternoon looking over my photographs and notes from my recent inspections and putting together repair estimates. The broken window was difficult because stained glass was a custom item. I looked up local artisans who did that sort of work and emailed them, asking for a quote. I sat back and stretched. It was a productive, if somewhat boring, afternoon.

It had been hard to focus on the task at hand. My mind kept wandering back to the murder. I had come no closer to answering the question of who would want to hurt Jim. There were a few possibilities but nothing concrete. And I couldn't figure out how it connected to Victor. While he was the medical examiner, I doubted he'd looked at the body yet, so it didn't seem like he could know anything that would endanger the killer.

I chewed on my lip and went through the list again. Gladys Palmer, the neighbor. Jay Mitchell, the son. Alex Sterling, the business partner. TwistedTales, the mysterious online contact. I sighed and pinched the bridge of my nose.

"I'm going to need to find something solid if I'm going to figure this one out."

Charlie chirped next to me, not even bothering to open his eyes.

"I know I'm stating the obvious." I stood.

He opened a single eye then curled into an even tighter ball, turning his back on me.

"Thanks for the vote of confidence." I chuckled and packed up my bag.

When I grabbed his leash, Charlie stood, stretched, and pranced toward me, his tail held high. I clipped him in, and together, we walked out to the car. He sat primly in his seat, staring out the window as we drove through town. As we passed the pier, he stood up on his hind legs and braced himself against the armrest as he stared out at the sea.

"Did you see something?" I asked.

He chirped.

I circled back around the block and parked near the entrance to the pier. I stared out at the boardwalk. The cold weather had chased most people inside, and without the space heaters going at full blast, it was especially cold out. The wind came in off the water and gusted across the wooden planks, making the thin layer of the leaves and pine needles airborne. They spun about before being deposited a few feet away, only to be picked up again by the next blast.

I zipped up my coat and pulled my collar up around my neck. Charlie curled up in his seat and closed his eyes. I chuckled, and he squeezed them shut. He clearly didn't want to be out in this weather any more than I did. I readied myself then darted out of my car into the chilly air.

The wind bit into my skin the instant I stepped outside. I squinted, my eyes stinging from the cold. I bent my head forward and trudged toward the pier. It was as empty as I'd expected. There wasn't a soul in sight as I marched up and down, my head swiveling from side to side as I tried to figure out what Charlie had noticed.

I gritted my teeth as I walked past the spot where I'd first noticed the body. Over the years, I had seen a lot of things as a claims adjuster, usually what was left behind after a body had been moved. Actually seeing a body in person was unsettling. I paused before I crossed that spot again. The benches hadn't been moved back yet. They were still all down on the beach. I stamped my feet and looked around, trying to find something—anything—that could help. My gaze passed over the crab banner that had half blown down in the wind more than once before I stopped and stared at the image. It had eyes.

A grin broke out across my face. The crab had eyes, and the night of the murder, it would have stared straight down at where I stood. I shuffled toward it and lifted the corner of the banner. My heart sank as I took it in. The banner was half down because it had torn during the windstorm. There was a tear straight across the image of the crab, bisecting its eyes. I pursed my lips and studied it. *Maybe the spell would still work?* I looked around one last time. The pier was still empty. Most of the shops had closed early for the day or had temporarily shuttered their doors for the season. There was no one out and about to see me.

I fumbled with my purse, pulled out my grandmother's first notebook, and flipped to a familiar page. It was for the spell that accessed the memory of an object. Symbolism was important. To see as the object, the object itself had to metaphorically see, as well—either through a camera lens or through the image of an eye. I read through the spell to remind myself of the incantation. It had been a few weeks since I had last practiced it. Once I held the words firmly in my head, I closed the notebook and held up the banner.

I stared straight into the torn crab's eyes and whispered the words of the spell under my breath. Motes of light spilled out of my mouth and swirled around me in a flurry. I raised my hand, and they settled around my fingertips as I brushed them against the banner. The lights sank into the artwork then vanished.

I blinked.

Nothing happened.

A spell had gone off, but I saw nothing.

I gritted my teeth, retrieved the notebook from my bag, and tried again. I held the book up next to the image. My gaze flicked between the spell and the image as I whispered the words again. More motes of light spiraled around me, settled at my fingertips, then vanished the second I touched the eyes. *Is it because it's torn?*

I shook out my hand and tried again. This time, I placed my fingertips against the mouth of the crab. The faint taste of sea salt lingered in my tongue as the scent of s'mores filled my nose. It was like my nose and mouth were back at that night. I played through it. The salt never left my mouth, but the scent of s'mores faded as it was replaced with sea salt and fish. Through the memory recall spell, I could taste that night. I could smell that night. But I could not see it. I groaned in frustration. *When would tasting a killer be helpful?*

I dropped the edge of the banner and backed away. I spun in place, searching for any other image with an eye or a camera that pointed in the right direction. There were several, but none of them pointed where I needed them to point. They all pointed farther down the pier or out to the Puget Sound.

I shoved the notebook back into my bag and stomped back to the car. I had been out in the cold long enough and had only hit dead ends.

Charlie perked up when I flopped down next to him. I flung my bag down onto the floorboards. He rested his chin on my arm and stared up at me, purring.

I stroked his soft fur and leaned back into my seat. "It was a good idea. But no cigar."

He headbutted me gently and crawled into my lap. I petted him as my mind worked. There had to be a way for me to see what had happened that night. *There has to.*

My phone dinged in my pocket. I fished it out as Charlie slipped out of my lap and curled back up in his favorite spot in the passenger seat.

> **GRACE:**
> I spoke to Agnes. You were right. She found my pile of questions overwhelming.

> **DANI:**
> I'm sorry, honey.

> **GRACE:**
> It's okay. I'm glad I checked before I got too much farther into it. She took all my sticky notes, though, and said she would work on a lesson plan with Sarah.

> **DANI:**
> That's great news!

> **GRACE:**
> I got worried they might start putting me off again though, so I got her to agree to set a date for our first session. It's going to be in three days, 8 am sharp.

> **DANI:**
> I'll be there.

I slipped my phone back into my pocket and started the engine. At least one of us had been lucky. Hopefully, tomorrow would prove to be more fruitful.

CHAPTER 8

The next morning was a flurry of activity. I spent most of it scampering across rooftops or shimmying under houses to peek into crawl spaces. The winter storm had torn across the island, leaving blown-over fences, downed tree limbs, and standing water in its wake. The day was unusually warm, which tended to happen after a deluge of water. I didn't need my coat, just a hoodie and a knit cap to keep the cold at bay.

I stopped by the Bizzy Bean on my way back to the office. The line snaked down the full length of the counter and around the plexiglass enclosure for the cats. It ended at the front door. I slipped inside and inched forward with the line as I went through my to-do list for the day. I pulled out my pocket notebook and checked off the items I'd already done. I had two more inspections to do, as well as downloading all those photos from my camera. It was going to be a late night.

I was still staring at my to-do list when I almost walked right into the Retirees. Their usual table was taken by a group of interns, and they stood there with exaggerated forlorn expressions on their faces. I tried not to chuckle as they turned toward me in unison.

"It's busy here today," I said.

"It's like the whole town decided it needed coffee." Betty sighed.

"It's not even that cold out," Agnes said.

Sarah crossed her arms. "Cold enough. I don't want to sit outside."

"Is there another event or something?" I asked, looking around. It really was like the whole town had come in for coffee. In the few minutes I had been in line, people had piled up behind me. The line now extended out the doors. I lost track of it as it wound down the block past the front windows.

"You haven't heard?" Betty perked up. She always enjoyed it when she knew something someone else didn't.

"Well, she's been working all day. Who would have told her?" Sarah reached out and pulled a twig from my hair.

"Told me what?" I tried to keep the exasperated tone out of my voice. The more rankled I was, the longer they drew things out. I forced a smile onto my face. *Remember. They are running the witch's school for Grace.* My patience was thinner than usual. I hadn't slept well the night before. Again.

"The Mayor—" Agnes inched in, her eyes twinkling with excitement.

"Pro tem," Sarah corrected.

Agnes frowned. "He won the election."

"True, but he doesn't officially start as mayor until January. He's still pro tem." Sarah crossed her arms.

"Technically." Betty rolled her eyes.

I couldn't help but chuckle. They were a lively lot who constantly bickered, but I couldn't imagine seeing them apart. Not for long. They lived and breathed town gossip together.

"As I was saying." Agnes playfully batted Sarah away. "The mayor decided it would be a good idea to hold a vigil. The awful business surrounding Jim's body being stolen has everyone on edge. And vigils bring people together."

A vigil? My eyes widened as the possibilities played through my head. A vigil would attract a lot of attention. But it was also an event that his close friends and family would be at. I could almost guarantee the killer would be there as well. I pulled out my notebook and reviewed my to-do list.

"What time is it at?" I asked.

"Officially…" Agnes began.

"It starts at sunset." Sarah followed her, as if it was one smooth sentence.

"But people are already gathering," Betty finished.

I nodded. The inspections were nonnegotiable, but everything else could move. An opportunity to see all the suspects in one place would not come again.

"Thanks, ladies." I stuffed my notebook back into my pocket and shuffled forward to keep my spot in line.

The line moved at a steady clip. Heather didn't have time to chat when I got up there to order my drink, so I promised to catch up with her later and headed out with a fresh cup of her honey-roasted brew.

I popped by the office on my way back out to pick up an extra card for my camera. I didn't want to miss the opportunity to take photos of the vigil.

I finished work just in time to make it to the vigil. I wound my way through downtown, looking for a space to park. Almost every spot was taken. I found a place to park four blocks from the pier. I jogged there. The movement helped keep me warm against the chill. The temperature had dropped when the sun went down.

The pier looked similar to the night of the winter kickoff event. Space heaters had been set up, lining the boardwalk. Benches had been gathered from the beach and lined the walkway. A large photo of Jim hung over the miniature stage at the end of the pier. I hadn't gotten a good look at him in person, but over the past two days, I had pored through his social media, which made him feel familiar. Despite his age, most of his hair was still a dark brown. He had combed it straight back, accentuating his pronounced widow's peak. It looked like the photographer had caught him midlaugh. The photo had the air of a candid shot, but it was too in focus and perfect to have been random.

I wandered through the crowd, my camera hanging around my neck. I examined the faces of the crowd as I moved. Almost the entire town had shown up. Every business owner from Marine View Drive was there. Nearly everyone from the local sheriff's department, including Peggy, weaved their way through the throng of people, their eyes alert and scanning the group. *Looks like they had a similar idea.* I made my way over to Chris.

He loomed over the crowd, his eyes constantly moving. He smiled widely as he noticed me winding my way through the people to him. My heart fluttered. While I had sometimes questioned my decision to get a divorce from Ed, in moments like this, I was glad I had. In the almost twenty years we had been married, not once had he looked that excited to see me. And that included our wedding day.

Chris moved to join me. The crowd parted around us, and I stepped in close.

"Why am I not surprised to see you here?" He drew me into a hug. "You're almost as bad as the Retirees."

I elbowed him in the rib. "What's that supposed to mean?"

He chuckled and stepped back. "Are you going to deny that town gossip makes you curious?" He lowered his voice. "Especially when crime is involved?"

I screwed my nose up at him. "And here I thought we were going to have a sweet moment."

He pulled me back into a hug. "Who says it can't be both?"

I settled into him. Inside his embrace, my worries from

the day melted away. I exhaled, and the tension in my shoulders I hadn't realized I'd been holding released. I leaned back and looked around the crowd. "Okay. I admit it. I'm here because of the town gossip. And crime."

"It's pretty tame so far," he said.

I looped my arm through his. I slid my hand up to my camera and snapped a few shots as we strolled through the crowd together.

"Are you on duty?" I asked.

He coughed and ran his hand through his hair. "Yes."

"Are you going to get in trouble for fraternizing with the enemy?"

He shrugged. "I don't care anymore, remember? If Bob extends my Miller Farm punishment, all that means for me is more coffee with you, right?"

"Right." I nodded and fought to keep my expression bland. It was childish of Bob to make Chris go sit out at the intersection that led to Miller's Farm at five in the morning for no reason. It wasn't like many people drove out that way. And it was never close enough for him to catch who was painting their cow blue anyway. I did the mental math. His next shift there was coming up soon. It was the same day as the witch's school. *I can do both.* He squeezed my hand. I stared up at him as we made our way to the end of the pier. *I can have both.*

We paused at the end of the pier and looked out of the crowd. I took a few more pictures. There were so many people there, I wasn't sure how useful my foray would actually be. They were all grouped together, almost like high school cliques. Peppered throughout the crowd, I recognized faces. There were at least twenty of Jim's coworkers, including Emily and Alex. They stood near the Crab Shack, their faces somber. There was something performative about it. The sadness didn't reach Alex's eyes.

Close to them was a group of men and women from his

neighborhood. Or at least, I assumed as much. They were all dressed professionally. The women wore dresses, along with sensible heels, and the men wore tailored pants with button-up shirts. Gladys and Mabel stood at opposite ends of the group. Gladys hugged a cardigan to her boxy frame, while Mabel was covered in a faux-fur coat that went all the way down to her ankles.

Not far from them were the interns. Jay stood in the center, with Ethan at his side. The group was young. They huddled together in two rings that ebbed and flowed into each other. The center ring was somber and consoling. They reached out and touched Jay and spoke to each other in whispered tones. The outer ring faced outward, eyes hard and glaring at the crowd—almost daring someone insincere to come up. For someone who wasn't officially an intern, he had made fast friends in the group.

The last group consisted of the business owners from downtown. They all knew each other from the various community planning events that the newly elected mayor, Steven Bishop, had planned over the past few months. His efforts to revitalize the downtown had really brought them together. While not business owners, the Retirees stood with that group. One of them chaired, or cochaired, most of the committees.

I took photos of each of the groups. There wasn't much movement between them. Friends tended to band together. Once each of them had formed around a landmark on the pier, they didn't move far. It was easy to spot the people who moved through the crowd—the sheriff, Deputy Harrison Abbott, Peggy, and a woman wearing a red peacoat.

I narrowed in on her and took another photo.

"You see something?" Chris asked.

"Maybe?" *Leave it to him to notice my change in demeanor.*

He squeezed my hand and let me go. "Don't do anything dangerous this time."

I turned and gave him one last hug then disappeared into the crowd. I felt his eyes follow me as I moved through the crowd and came to a stop near the group of neighbors. The woman had sidled up to them and wormed her way inside the group. I fiddled with my phone and listened in.

"I know. It's just heartbreaking. I didn't know him for long. Do you know if they have any leads yet?" The woman had a deeper, raspy voice with a sultry edge that reminded me of lounge singers.

"I don't know how serious the sheriff is taking it, to be honest," Mabel said. "They haven't even come by to question me, and I'm his neighbor."

I covered my mouth to hide my smile. It was clear Mabel had been a queen bee for so long that she struggled when she wasn't in the spotlight.

Gladys snorted. "So am I. And I knew him better than you. Trust me, they came by, all right. Asking all the wrong questions too."

"Were they asking you about that tree?" a man asked.

Tree? What tree? I inched closer, my eyes focused on my phone as I eavesdropped. *Is that what their feud is about? Who gets into a feud over a tree?*

"That tree?" Gladys stomped her foot. "That tree was planted on my property the day my sister was born. It's practically part of the family."

I pecked out a note to myself on my phone. *Look into tree dispute.*

"Sounds like they were asking the right questions to me." Mabel crossed her arms.

"Now, Mabel—" the man began.

"It sounds like you didn't like him much, ma'am," the woman in the peacoat said.

"I don't care for that tone." Gladys glowered at her. "I don't like many people, but that doesn't mean I'm a killer."

They studied each other as the silence stretched out

66

between them. After almost a minute, the woman in the red peacoat let out an awkward laugh and said goodbye to the group before moving onto another one.

I followed along behind her. She went from group to group, chatting for a few minutes. At each one, she would finally ask the question that was on everybody's mind: Do they have any suspects yet? Every group said no but had different theories. None of them sounded solid.

After the woman had made it through all the groups, she backed up against the old arcade. She studied the crowd, her eyes lingering on the interns, then she ducked around the corner. I followed her, working hard to keep my distance without losing track of her movements. Ever since my run-in with the private investigator Derrick Miller, I had been working on my tailing skills. It was embarrassing that he noticed me so quickly. YouTube was a wonderful rabbit hole of information. I really could learn almost anything there.

She crossed the parking lot and walked half a block up before getting into a black Toyota Corolla. I walked in front of her car and stopped at one of the meters. I fed coins into the machine as I watched her out of the corner of my eye. She typed out a message on her phone before starting her engine. She didn't even look in my direction. I snapped a photo of her car, focusing in on the license plate, then made my way back up the pier.

I couldn't follow her. I would stand out too much on these empty streets. But luckily, I could find her car later with a tracking spell.

CHAPTER 9

I groaned and rolled over to turn off my alarm. The vigil had ended very late, making it impractical to track the woman down. I didn't want to miss anything, though, so I had set my alarm for well before sunrise so I could find her car before she got moving for the day. I rolled out of bed. Charlie yawned and followed suit. I wrapped myself up in a robe and shuffled toward the shower.

Instead of following me, Charlie sauntered down the hall and tapped his foot against Grace's door. Her light was still on. She opened it, and he ducked inside. I chuckled. *I guess that is one way to tell me it's too early.* He usually opted to go into the office with me, but on early days, he always wanted to go back to bed.

I held the robe tight around me and started the water. I had forgotten how chilly Gran's house could get in the winters. They had built the house in the early '20s, when insulation wasn't as popular. I mentally added "install new insulation" to my home renovation list as I shampooed my hair.

Grace's light was off when I emerged fifteen minutes later. I got dressed in dark jeans. I layered a flowy blouse over a tank top, pulled my winter coat over the top, and finished the look with a knit cap, gloves, and faux-fur-lined boots. Despite my best efforts, the boots were heavy, and I ended up clomping down the stairs.

Outside, frost clung to every surface, shimmering under the moonlight. The gravel crunched under my boots. Fortunately, it didn't take long for my car to become toasty. While it heated up, I got out the map of the island and laid it flat against the steering wheel. In one hand, I held my Gran's second notebook, and in the other, I held my phone with the photo of the car. I hadn't practiced this spell enough to remember it yet. I repeated the words in my head a few times. Once I could remember them without stumbling, I relaxed my eyes and stared blankly down at the map, whispering the words to the spell.

Like with all of my magic, motes of light fluttered out of my mouth. It danced between my phone and the map, swirling back and forth in smaller and smaller circles until the lights landed on a point just north of Point Pleasant. I lifted the map closer to my face.

Langley.

I let the spell go. The lights dissipated, leaving the car dark. I flipped to a map of Langley. I shook out my arms, placed the map back on the steering wheel, and started again.

It took two more times for me to narrow it down to the exact location. The mysterious woman was parked right along the water's edge at the Boatyard Inn. She had the air of an out-of-towner, so it made sense she was staying at a hotel —a swanky one, at that. I'd only been inside once. It had a wonderful mix of luxury and rustic island charm. I took the road, headed north out of town, and drove to Edgecliff Park, which was only a couple blocks away. I recast the spell. Her car hadn't moved.

I bought a coffee from a local Java Hut then circled the block a few times until I found a spot where I could sit, watch, and wait. I pulled out my phone to put on an audio-book to pass the time then paused. My lock screen was a photo of me, Grace, and Heather. After things had settled down after the last investigation and it had become clear that Grace really was here to stay, Heather had made a cake to celebrate. She'd made two cakes actually—one for us and a cat-friendly one for Charlie and Star. We had clustered together to take the photo. Charlie's stuck out. He sat in the middle of the group, his face covered in cat-safe frosting, and his blue eyes wide in surprise. It had been a good day. Grace needed to know she was welcome and loved, even after dropping out of university unexpectedly. Heather had always been good at making people feel at home.

I chewed on my lip. I had promised Heather to be safe. And here I was, doing a stakeout without backup. I texted her, telling her where I was and what I was doing. It only took a few seconds for bubbles to appear to show she was typing. I held my breath, watching them appear and disappear. She was probably mad I hadn't given her more notice.

HEATHER:
Okay.

I stared at the word. My heart clenched. It wasn't like I could explain how I'd found the mysterious woman or why I hadn't invited Heather along. I contemplated responding and giving her more information, but there wasn't much to tell yet. I shoved my phone into my pocket and sat in silence, staring at my rearview mirror until the woman emerged from her hotel almost an hour later.

I ran through the tips and tricks I had learned over the past month on how to follow people. Before she left the parking lot, I whispered the spell for heightening my senses. All the advice said to hang far enough back that I could still see the target. This spell would hopefully give me an edge. I winced as the sounds of the bay and the pressure of my knit cap overwhelmed me. Someday I was going to find a way to heighten only one of my senses at a time, instead of all of them then shutting them down one by one.

The woman drove past me and headed out of town. I waited until she reached the end of the block then followed her. I kept her in view, even as the cars slowly built up between us. She drove with the flow of traffic, about five miles over the speed limit. I trailed her through Langley then out onto the road, headed toward Point Pleasant.

I snorted. *Just my luck. I could have waited in town.*

She pulled into a parking spot outside the Slice of Life Diner and walked inside. I circled the block to find a good vantage point. As I passed the diner a second time, Alex got out of his car and walked into the diner as well. *What's the likelihood that two suspects are in the same place at the same time?* I drummed my fingers against the steering wheel as I debated my options. The diner was a public space. *It wouldn't be odd for me to go in. And I might hear something useful.*

I parked two doors down and walked up to the diner. We were headed into winter, so the menu had shifted. Willow's classic apple pie milkshake was a staple, but it had been joined by a white chocolate orange creamsicle shake. My mouth watered as I entered.

The mystery woman sat perched at the counter. Alex had taken a seat next to her. They were facing forward, but in the reflection in the glass over the counter, I saw their mouths move. They were talking.

I took a seat at a table nearby. It was just before the breakfast rush. The sun had only been up for half an hour. Even so, the space was still filled with the sounds of clinking cutlery and murmured conversations. I ordered quickly and settled in. I gritted my teeth, mentally preparing myself for the onslaught of sensations, as I whispered the words for the heightened senses spell again. The motes of light swirled around me, settling into my skin.

I gripped the bench beneath me as everything came into sharp focus. A wave of weariness hit me. I hadn't cast this many spells in a row in a while. A small tear, too small for the human eye to see, cut into the side of my palm. I closed my eyes against the bright lights and colors from all the photos decorating the walls. I concentrated, willing the unneeded senses away, until only sound remained.

It was as if I were at a concert. Everything was loud, from the hum of the lights and the sizzling of bacon to the sounds of thirty people chewing and talking all at once. I tilted my head toward the counter and tried to focus on the mystery woman's conversation.

"You're behind on your payments," the woman said.

Ice clinked into a glass, drowning out Alex's response.

"That's not my problem. I completed the job." Gone were the sultry undertones. It had been replaced with something colder. Her words were harsh and guttural.

"I can't move funds like that right now. Someone would notice."

The woman pushed her plate across the counter and stood. She wiped her mouth and threw her napkin down onto her plate. "A contract is a contract. Don't make me enforce it."

She stalked away from him and disappeared through the restroom door. He slumped into his chair, cursing under his breath. He fished his wallet out of his pants, threw a few dollars down onto the counter, and strode outside.

I looked between the bathroom door and Alex's departing form. My food hadn't come yet, but she could leave at any moment. I dropped the spell and scurried out of the booth to the cash register. Willow stood behind the counter. She had one pen behind her ear and another in her hand that she chewed on between writing notes. As I approached, she looked up and beamed at me. I came to a stop in front of her and gave her a sheepish smile. She was dressed in her classic bohemian style, with her strawberry-blond hair piled on top of her head in a messy bun. She pushed her red-rimmed glasses up.

"Gingerbread, eggnog, or sugar cookie?" she asked, tapping her pen against the notepad. "I can't decide."

"What's this for?" I asked.

"Next week's special."

"Are you taking a poll?"

She cocked her head to one side and grinned. "I wasn't. But that's a great idea. You can be the first vote."

"Eggnog," I said. "And I hate to do this, but I forgot about something at the office. Could I get my food to go instead?"

"Sure thing." She jotted down my vote then rang me up.

I shuffled from foot to foot, my eyes flicking between Willow and the ladies' room while she packaged up my food. Behind me, a large group of winter interns were gathering up their belongings. The restroom door opened, and the women stepped out.

"Hey, before you go," Willow called over to the interns, "I'm taking a poll."

The woman looked right at me as Willow handed me my food order. Our eyes met, and a look of recognition crossed her face. I grabbed my bag and ducked out as the interns gave their votes.

Holding my food bag, I hurried away from the diner. The door opened behind me, and I glanced over my shoulder as the woman stepped out onto the sidewalk. She crossed her arms. I focused on the sidewalk in front of me as the hairs on the back of my neck stood up. *Did she see my car earlier? I hung back, but I don't know. Just act natural. Keep walking.* The interns piled out onto the street after the woman. I slowed my pace and joined their group as they strolled down the street.

The group of interns chatted away. Their excitement was infectious. There was a heated debate over the virtues of eggnog over sugar cookies. They did not even mention gingerbread. I fiddled with my bag. At the next intersection, I took a quick peek over my shoulder. The woman had either gone back inside or returned to her car. She wasn't out on the street anymore.

As I waited for the light to change, Ethan stepped up next to me. I hadn't noticed him in the crowd. Surrounded by all these people, he seemed out of his element. He collapsed in on himself, his already scrawny shoulders rounded inward.

"You're Dani, aren't you?" he asked, running his hands through his unkempt brown hair.

"Yeah," I said. "Can I help you?"

He smiled. It warmed up his face, making him seem younger, almost boyish somehow, as his cheeks dimpled. "I don't know, ma'am. I've just been hearing about you all over town. Word is you're some sort of investigator. Is that right?" He fiddled with the pair of headphones as he spoke.

I tried not to laugh. In a small town like Point Pleasant, anyone could become part of the town's gossip. Even me. "I wouldn't say that. I'm a claims adjuster."

"So you didn't solve Jessica's murder?" he asked.

I blinked, not expecting that to still be part of the rumor mill. "I might have helped some—"

"Or Tina's?"

I fidgeted with my food bag. My phone chimed in my bag. The hairs on my arm stood up. I tried to focus on the sensation. *Am I cold, or was that a sign?* I wasn't really paying attention to Ethan as I answered. "I might have helped with that one too."

He nodded, pressing his lips together.

"Why do you ask?" I asked.

"It's probably nothing."

The light changed, and the group moved across the street. He faltered before following.

"That doesn't sound like nothing."

74

"I wouldn't want to get anyone in trouble." He looked back the way we'd come. "I should probably head back. Victor's waiting."

My phone chimed in my pocket again. The hairs on my arms rose again. I reached into my pocket and gripped my phone. The pressure in the back of my head built. *That's a sign.*

I pulled it out and froze. It was a notification from that dating app I had downloaded. TwistedTales had sent me two messages.

"Is it something important?" he asked, peering over my shoulder.

> **TWISTEDTALES:**
> I saw you following me.
>
> Why are you looking into Jim's death?

I swallowed. "I should probably get this."

His face fell. "Yeah, I understand."

He turned to walk away. I reached out toward him. He stopped, with my hand hovering over his shoulder.

"Look—it's Ethan, right?" I asked.

He nodded.

"I'm sorry. But I've really got to get this. But I think we should talk. I'm a good sounding board, if nothing else. When I'm not being pulled in a hundred different directions. Let's get coffee together later. Okay?" I took out a business card and thrust it into his hands.

He shrugged but took the card. "If I've got time."

He took another step toward the intersection but was forced to stop by the red light. I didn't want to push it, so I let him stand there. *Did I just miss an opportunity?* My phone dinged again, sending another shiver down my arm. *All right. I've got it. I need to talk to this woman.* I turned toward my office and opened the app.

> **TWISTEDTALES:**
> We should meet. I've got information for
> you. And I can guarantee you, it's not what
> you think.

I chewed on my lip, standing there in the middle of the sidewalk. *TwistedTales? It must be our mystery woman. What am I supposed to think it is?*

> **DANI:**
> Okay. When and where?

> **TWISTEDTALES:**
> The Pier. 8 a.m. tomorrow morning.
>
> Come alone.

My heart clenched at that last sentence. Heather would be furious with me if I went alone. She would insist on coming. *But the woman spotted my tail. Could I even bring backup without her noticing? Maybe if I tell Heather right before it goes down? She'll be nearby but not there to be seen. It's still keeping my promise.*

> **DANI:**
> I'll be there.

I pocketed my phone. The light changed behind me, and traffic flowed by. It was going to be a long day. I turned back to Ethan, but he was already crossing the street, his hands shoved into his pockets and headphones covering his ears. I cradled my breakfast and walked the rest of the way to the office. At least I had a lot of claims to keep me busy.

CHAPTER 10

I tossed and turned all night, struggling to sleep as the case rattled through my mind. Every time I asked myself why I was so invested, Victor's face floated through my thoughts. I rolled over and stared at my alarm clock until I finally fell asleep well after two a.m. When seven o'clock rolled around, I struggled to get out of bed. In my sleep, I had become tangled up in my blankets. A weight had settled over my whole body. My head pounded from lack of sleep and using so much magic the day before. I pushed the blankets aside and got up to go through the motions. My stomach was too unsettled to eat anything.

It was still dark out when I left the house. I drove on autopilot to the pier and parked in the empty parking lot. I was about ten minutes early. The sky was lightening at the horizon, teasing the arrival of the sun. Bleary-eyed, I leaned back in my seat to wait. My stomach was still doing somersaults, and the chill had crept into the car. The hairs along my arms stood up under my jacket as a shiver went through my body. *Another sign?* I shifted in my seat, trying to focus on the feeling, but my mind was sluggish, and the sensation was gone before I could figure it out.

The sky turned pink along the water. I yawned, stretched, and shuffled out of the car. The wind caught my car door, ripping it out of my hand. It slammed next to me. I jumped at the loud sound.

"Easy, Dani," I muttered to myself. "It's just a meeting."

I turned back toward the pier and froze. A dark shape darted off the boardwalk then froze at the edge of the sidewalk. The hairs on the back of my neck stood on end as the figure stared right at me. My heart leaped into my throat, and I stumbled back. They turned and sprinted away from me. In the dim light, all I could tell was that it was a person. The pressure in the back of my head increased as my Sight screamed at me. I cursed under my breath. I had been too tired to read the signals. Surging forward, I whispered the words to the enhanced senses spell. The weight of exhaustion still clung to my body. The motes of lights stuttered and went out before they settled onto my skin.

I skidded to a stop before I reached the wooden planks, my heart pounding. Wide-eyed, I scanned the surrounding area. I was very much alone—and vulnerable. I backpedaled to my car and locked the doors once I was inside. *What if they come back? Who was that? Why am I so scared?*

My hands trembled as I pulled out my phone. I needed backup. I punched in Heather's number. She picked up on the third ring.

"Heather, I'm at the pier to meet a witness, and I saw someone running away, and... I don't know what to do. I think something bad happened."

"You... you promised!" she sputtered. Her voice rose on the last word. I had never heard fury in her voice before.

"I know. I just... I didn't think." The last word came out as a mumble. I had thought about calling her and had decided not to. I hung my head.

"Did you see who they were?" she asked.

I shook my head and stopped. She wasn't with me to see it. "No."

I leaned forward in my seat and squinted at the pier. It was empty that time of morning. There was no movement.

The witness. I chewed on my lip and pushed open my car door. I crept forward, my eyes darting from side to side as I made my way toward the pier.

"Why does it sound like you're outside now?"

"I've got you on the line. That counts as being safe, right?"

"Dani!" she squealed. Her hand muffled her next words. "I'm headed out. If anyone else comes in, let them know I'll be back in five. No. Make that fifteen."

I continued creeping forward. The wooden planks creaked under me. I rounded the corner and inched forward, one small step at a time.

At the top of the stairs, there was a dark mass. I tiptoed toward it, clutching my phone. Heather muttered to herself on the other end as she stomped down the sidewalk toward the pier. She was still a few blocks out. I could wait. But I couldn't help myself. My curiosity pulled me forward until the dark mass took form.

It was a body.

I gasped and dropped my phone.

"Dani!" Heather screamed into the phone.

I crouched and picked it up. "I'm fine. Heather, I… I think someone killed the witness."

"Don't you dare—"

I hung up and dialed 9-1-1.

I was still on the phone with 9-1-1 when Heather sprinted up the boardwalk toward me. She skidded to a stop next to me. Her head swiveled from side to side as she took in the scene, her green eyes wide. She tucked her braid behind her shoulder and stalked the last few feet to me. She crossed her arms and glowered at me until the sirens began wailing in the distance. Her eyes flicked between me and the

79

body, and her expression softened. She wrapped her arms around me as I hung up the phone.

I buried my face in her shoulder. I trembled against her, and she squeezed me until I calmed down. There was something comforting about the pressure. We stood there for a few minutes in silence before she spoke.

"Who is it?" she asked, her voice muffled by my coat.

"TwistedTales. I don't remember her actual name." I pulled back and wiped my eyes. My whole body trembled as I took a faltering step toward the body and kneeled next to it. The mystery woman stared up at me blankly. "I found her online. TwistedTales was her username."

Heather put her hand on my shoulder. Her body twisted away from me so she didn't have to see.

A sheriff's car pulled up at the end of the pier, and Chris jumped out. He ran toward me. A few seconds later, a second cruiser arrived, and Harrison and Bob got out. Harrison marched down the pier while Bob slowly moved to the trunk of his car and picked up a duffle bag.

Heather moved away from me as Chris came to a stop next to me. He drew me into a hug.

"I'm sorry," I murmured into his chest. My fingers curled into his shirt as I clutched onto him. My mind whirled. *The woman might have been alive when I got here. If I had only... only what?* I fumbled with what to say or think. I breathed in deeply. Chris's sandalwood aftershave filled my nose. *If only I had been with you.* "I'm sorry I missed our coffee date."

He squeezed me tightly. "Like I'm worried about coffee. What were you even doing out here?"

"I was on my way into the Bizzy Bean to get coffee when I saw someone running away from the pier. See something, say something, right? It looked suspicious. I couldn't help myself. You know me. I had to check it out." I peered at Heather, pleading with my eyes. The sheriff was coming, and I didn't want to admit I was investigating another murder. He would only see it as me interfering with the case.

She shook her head.

I mouthed the word *please* at her.

"I made her promise to call me if she was doing anything dumb. And she did." Heather glared and crossed her arms. "I told her not to get out of the car until I got there, but she didn't listen."

I mouthed the word *please* at her again.

"With everything going on, I didn't want her chasing after some random person. I will never understand her insistence on running straight at the danger."

"So, you saw someone running away from the pier and decided to check it out?" Chris pulled back, his hand smoothing down my hair as he studied my face.

"Yeah," I said.

"Yep. That's about it." Heather snorted.

Harrison cleared his throat. He stood, hovering a few feet away.

Bob was close behind, holding a giant roll of caution tape. "Mark off the perimeter," Bob said, thrusting the tape toward Harrison.

Harrison nodded and trotted off with the tape in hand. He was the tallest of the three men, at about six and a half feet. While he normally slouched, his lanky arms and legs dangling down, today, he stood fully erect as he moved around the crime scene, taping it off.

"Ms. Williams," Bob said. He lengthened the word *miss*, his disapproval clear in his voice. "Imagine seeing you here."

"Better her than Martha." Heather stepped in close, slipping her arm around mine. We linked arms as she tilted her head back. Heather stared down her nose at Bob. "Or would you prefer poor Mrs. Foster finding a dead body outside the Crab Shack when she comes in? It would probably give her another heart attack."

Bob shuffled under the weight of Heather's gaze. He cleared his throat and looked away. "We're going to need a full statement."

The white panel van of the coroner's office pulled up at the end of the pier. Victor and Ethan climbed out. Victor pulled his tailcoat closed around him and buttoned it up as he strode toward us. Ethan shuffled along next to him, wearing an oversized puffy jacket.

I stared at Victor, my eyes widening as he got closer. My body shook. The vision of his death was still present, but instead of shifting between a hundred different injuries, now it shifted slowly between three—like his fate was closer and closer to being sealed.

"I'll handle that," Chris said to Bob, pulling me in close.

With Heather on one side and Chris on the other, my trembling slowed. I blinked back tears. *Have I done something to make it more certain?*

"Of course you will." Bob snorted. "Be sure to take better notes this time."

I shuffled between Heather and Chris to his car. I hovered next to his car as he took a seat and started the engine.

Heather held out her hand. "Your keys."

"What?"

"He can drop you off at your house. And I'll bring you your car."

"I can just come back for it."

She narrowed her eyes and stepped in closer. "No. You promised me. And this is the only way I can guarantee you'll talk to me about what's going on before you run off again. Your keys."

"Is this—"

"Just because I covered for you this time doesn't mean I'm going to continue to do so without an explanation." She thrust her hand out farther. "Your keys. Now."

I fished them out of my pocket and dropped them into her hand.

She turned on her heel and stormed off down the boardwalk.

"Hey!" Bob yelled. "We need a statement from you too."

"It's not like you don't know where to find me, Bob. I've got work to do!" Heather yelled over her shoulder.

I winced. She was normally a sweetheart. It looked like I had finally pushed her too far. I hung my head and lowered myself into the cruiser next to Chris. He reached across the seats and squeezed my hand.

"You don't have to do this now," he said.

"No. Let's get this out of the way." I squeezed his hand back. "Although next time we have a coffee date, I'm going to hope for something a little less exciting."

He shook his head, laughter in his eyes, then put his car into gear. We drove into the station in a companionable silence.

CHAPTER 11

It took over an hour to give my statement to Chris. I repeated it a few times, and he jotted down every word I said. I chided myself for not eating breakfast before I headed out. If I had been well rested, if I had food in my stomach, maybe I could have cast that spell and made out who'd run away from the pier. We finally stopped when my stomach grumbled so loudly the recorder picked it up.

Chris drove me home as promised. I barely looked up as we pulled in. I sat there, fumbling with my seat belt. He had to get back to the station, but I lingered in the car, wanting to stretch out our time together as much as I could.

"They're tenacious, aren't they?" Chris chuckled.

"What?" I blinked.

He nodded toward a pickup truck parked in my driveway. It was Betty's truck. My heart skipped a beat. *The school...*

He leaned forward and peered up at my dining-room window. Seated around the table were Grace, Sarah, Betty, and Agnes. "I'm sure the news is all over town. Looks like they are here to get the news straight from the source."

I forced a laugh. "You're probably right." I squeezed his

hand one last time and ducked out of the car. "I shouldn't keep them waiting."

I lingered in the driveway, waving as he reversed and disappeared into the tree line. I trudged up the front steps and leaned my head against the front door. Weariness settled over me. I had already disappointed one friend for the day. Hopefully, Grace would understand. I pushed the door in and stepped into the living room.

The voices in the other room stopped, and Grace poked her head out the door. "We were beginning to think you'd forgotten."

I shuffled forward, my head still bent down, and pulled her into a hug. "It was a rough morning." I choked on my words.

"What happened?" Betty asked. The Retirees had stood from their places around the table.

"There was another murder this morning." The words came out jumbled as the stress of the morning came to the surface.

I was always a crier. Anger, frustration, sadness, or stress would push me over the edge into crying territory. I had tried to work on it over the past few years, but the stress of the week had finally bubbled over. I couldn't hold it in anymore. The Retirees swarmed around Grace and me, forming a giant hug ball. They hugged me until I cried myself out.

Once the tears ended, they pulled away and glided back to their seats at the table, leaving me with Grace. I wiped away the tears. "Sorry about that, honey. I hope I didn't miss too much of the lesson."

I followed her to the table. The entire surface had been taken over by banker boxes and paper. The boxes were faded. With the lids off, there was a clear line dividing the white strip along to the top to the sun-bleached yellow of the bottom. I took a seat next to Agnes and picked up a piece of paper that was in front of my seat. It was a report card for Sarah from the second grade. Betty shoved a plate of scones toward me.

"What's all this?" I asked as I gratefully took a scone. Cream cheese and strawberry preserves sat next to the plate. I spread them both on thick and bit into the scone. I danced in my seat. It was still warm from the oven and absolutely delicious.

"I didn't really know where to start," Agnes began.

"We didn't have kids, so we didn't need to pass down our legacy," Betty continued.

"But I remember my mama teaching me when I was a kid," Sarah picked up.

Agnes took the report card from me and studied it. "And being a bit of a pack rat, she had stashed away all the lessons."

"If only we knew which box it was all in." Betty chuckled. "Is this the Christmas card I got for you in the seventh grade?"

Sarah crossed her arms. "I know it's in the boxes labeled 'school stuff.'"

"There are twenty of them." Agnes pulled out a photo album and shoved it to the side. "And I question the 'school stuff' label."

I helped them sort through the papers. It was a jumble of things Sarah had collected between the ages of six and fourteen. Most of it was schoolwork for elementary and middle school, but mixed in was the occasional assignment given to her by her mother. We piled it all together, one random piece of paper at a time.

As we worked, Grace flipped through the photo album. She paused at a page and sat staring down at it while we sorted through another box. After a few minutes of staring, she turned the album around. "Who are they?"

I leaned forward and studied the photo. It was a grainy black-and-white shot of a group of women. There were seven of them, all wearing knee-length pleated skirts with matching cloche hats. They sat, arms linked, on the pier, grinning at the camera. One of them looked familiar.

"That's my mother's coven." Sarah held out her hand.

Grace handed her the album.

"The group moved out here together," Agnes said. "They look so young."

"This was my mama, Hazel. This was Betty's mom, Bea. Technically, Betty is Beatrice Taylor the Sixth. This is your great-great-grandmother, Edie." Sarah pointed from face to face as she spoke.

I had never met Edie. She'd passed away a few years after I was born, but Gran had talked about her caring personality a lot when I visited as a kid. She'd said I reminded her of Edie. "This is Agnes's mother, Clara. And this is Lillian Jones and Ruby Miller. I'm not sure who the woman in the middle is. She wasn't part of the coven when I was growing up."

"Can I see?" Grace held out her hand for the album.

Sarah handed it back.

"Is it okay if I pull the photo out?" Grace asked.

"Go right ahead. Just be careful with it."

Grace gingerly pulled back the plastic film, removed the photo, and flipped it over. The writing was in pencil and had faded over the years. She squinted at it, trying to make out the letters. "Meredith Walker?" she whispered.

"I think that sounds right," Sarah said. "I think my mom mentioned her once or twice. But it's so long ago."

Grace continued to stare at the photo as we unpacked the rest of the boxes. Sarah handed me a few more papers to go through. She was still staring at it when we finished sorting through the pile of lessons Hazel had put together for her daughter. Sarah flipped through the lessons, organizing them by date. I studied Grace over the stack of papers in my hand. *What's so special about that photo?*

"Can I keep this?" Grace looked up from the photo. "It's

87

just so cool, looking at a piece of my family's history. You know?"

"You can borrow it. I'll want the album back," Sarah said.

Betty chuckled. "She's too much of a pack rat to let anything go for long."

Grace put the photo back and got up to stow the album in her room.

While she was out of the room, Betty leaned in close and stage-whispered at me, "So, when are you going to tell us about the dead body?"

Agnes glared at her. "Betty! Do you really want to bring that back up? Couldn't you see how traumatized she was when she got home?"

"You don't have to share anything with us, dear." Sarah reached over and squeezed my hand. "Unless you want to, of course."

Agnes glared at her too.

"What? I can't be curious?" Sarah threw her hands into the air.

Grace slunk back into the room and sat down at the edge of the table. The group looked at her and fell silent. Grace's eyes swiveled from person to person. "Don't hold back on my account. I'm curious too."

"Fine." Working through the piles of things had been meditative. It had helped me refocus my thoughts. "There isn't too much to tell. My biggest lead was killed this morning."

A shocked silence fell over the table, then Agnes leaned forward. "Who was it?"

I shook my head. "I don't remember her name. She showed up at the kickoff event, and I've seen her around town."

"What did she look like?" Betty asked. "We talked to everyone at the kickoff."

"And I've got the memory for names," Sarah said. "If she mentioned it, I'll know it."

"Pretty. Chestnut hair. I think she was wearing a red peacoat at the party."

They all nodded and began whispering to each other. I still couldn't figure out how they did it. They all talked at once but still somehow understood each other. They sat back, and Sarah turned toward me. "Natasha Steele."

"She never said what she did," Betty said. "But she flew in from Denver."

Agnes nodded. "She was sad that she wasn't going to get any skiing in. Not enough snow in the mountains yet."

It was anticlimactic. I had her name, but it was meaningless. I still knew nothing about her.

"I saw her around town, asking… questions similar to my own. At first, I thought she was a suspect, but then she said she had something for me. I was supposed to meet her this morning."

"And she was…?" Betty trailed off.

I nodded. "At the pier. I saw someone running away when I got there, but I didn't get a good look at them."

"What about that memory recall spell?" Grace asked. "There was that giant crab picture."

"I tried it, but the picture got damaged in the storm. It didn't work."

"Rats," the Retirees said in unison. They slumped in their seats.

"Who is still on your list?" Grace asked.

"The neighbor, Gladys. She had some sort of feud going with Jim over a tree." I ticked them off as I counted. "The business partner, Alex. He knew Natasha. I saw them meeting up. And maybe Jay? I should probably just take him off the list."

Gravel crunched in the driveway as a car pulled up outside. I stood and peeked out the window. It was Heather.

My shoulders curled inward at the sight of her. She slammed the car door and stalked toward the house, her back straight and her jaw set.

Heather knocked on the front door. The Retirees gathered up the boxes, quickly stowing away their contents.

"You can leave them here," Grace offered.

Sarah nodded. "We should set the next date. It'll take me a few days to look through the material and come up with my own lesson plan."

"Same time next week?" Betty asked.

Grace nodded and started carting the boxes to her room as I answered the front door.

"I was going to wait until the café closed," Heather said, stepping into the living room. "But with all this weather, I realized you probably need the car, and I was just being selfish. I'm still—" She faltered when she saw the Retirees clustered around the dining room table.

"We were just wrapping up," Betty said.

"Grace wanted to know more about her Gran," Agnes piped in.

"Thank you all for coming," Grace said as she lifted one of the last of the boxes. "I'm really excited to look through that album."

The Retirees said their goodbyes. Heather hovered awkwardly in the living room until they left. Charlie emerged from his cat bed in the window, yawning and stretching to see them off. He wound his way through Heather's legs, purring as he rubbed against her. Her icy exterior melted, and she kneeled to pick him up. She held him to her chest as she took a seat on the couch. She sat perched at the edge, her knees bent beneath her. Grace lingered in the dining room, slowly sorting the last of the paperwork.

I hovered in the doorway. *What do I tell her? We've never had a fight like this before.*

"I can't stay for too long. My winter intern will be here in a few minutes to pick me up."

I nodded and sat down at the other end of the couch. "Heather, I'm sorry. I... I got wrapped up in things and forgot to update you."

"Forgot to update me? Do you have any idea how scared I was? That could have been you!" Heather pushed her face into Charlie's fur. He placed his paws on the top of her head, purring into her ear.

"I didn't—"

"You promised. And on day one, you broke it." She lowered Charlie to her lap and glared at me. Her eyes were red rimmed. "Why do you even care so much about this one? I understood with Jessica. You knew her. I understood with Tina. It was connected to your job. But this. Do you just enjoy running into danger?"

"I..." I faltered, searching for an answer. "I'm just a curious person, I guess."

"A curious person? That woman died, Dani. Not just died. That woman was murdered. And it could have been you!"

"Just tell her the truth," Grace said from the doorway.

I spun in my seat. *How long had she been standing there?*

"Yes. The truth." Heather stood.

Charlie jumped from her arms. He walked from person to person, rubbing against our legs. It was like he was desperately telling us not to fight.

"I am," I spluttered.

"She has dreams." Grace crossed her arms and entered the room.

"Dreams?" Heather's head swiveled back and forth between us.

"Sometimes they come true," Grace continued.

"What is she talking about, Dani?" Heather looked at me, trying to hold my gaze.

"I... I don't know." I looked away.

"You don't know?" Heather tried to catch my eye again.

"Like I said. I'm just a curious person. I'm sorry I forgot to call you."

"You forgot?" Heather folded in on herself, hugging her arms to the stomach. "You don't forget things that are important to you."

I avoided looking at her. My heart clenched in my chest as tears threatened to come loose again.

"You're my best friend, Dani. And I thought I was yours." She stalked toward the door. She yanked it open and stepped outside. "I guess I was wrong."

My heart broke as she left. I stood and watched her as she trudged down the driveway to wait for her intern.

"I can't believe you." Grace stared at me.

"What am I supposed to tell her?"

"The truth." Grace shook her head. "It was wrong when Gran kept it from you. It was wrong when you kept it from me. And it's wrong now, too, and you know it."

"We're not supposed to—"

"It's not against the rules. Betty told me what the rules were. The greater witchy world just frowns on it. But they're not here. She is. You can tell her. You should tell her."

"What if she doesn't believe me?" I asked.

"Then make her. You should be able to be honest with the people who matter. She matters. She's your best friend. You need to tell her."

"Tell her I'm a witch? That I saw our friend die? That I keep seeing Victor—" I clasped my hands over my mouth.

"Keep seeing Victor? You've had another vision?" Grace crossed the room and peered into my face.

I nodded. "It's not certain, though. It keeps changing."

"Oh, Mom." She put her arms around me. "You've really got to stop bottling things up. I'm not a child anymore."

"You'll always be my baby," I said.

Grace chuckled. "There's a difference. This isn't a journey

you have to make on your own. If you're worried about Victor, then... let's talk about the visions. You might have missed something. And if not, we can drive by to check up on him. And while we do all that, you can think long and hard about how you are going to make things up to Heather."

"How did you get so wise? And demanding?" I wiped my eyes. It really had been a stressful few days.

"I learned from the best."

CHAPTER 12

I spent the next few hours going over my visions and reading through the notebooks with Grace to see if there was anything we could do. Periodically, one of us would cast the tracking spell on Victor. He was at the funeral home, always in a slightly different position, which gave us hope he was still alive.

After flipping through the second notebook for the fourth time, I flung it down on the kitchen counter and sighed. I pinched the bridge of my nose. "I don't think there's anything in here."

"He's moved from the basement to the living room." Grace looked up from our sketch of the funeral home.

I glanced out the window. The sun had set twenty minutes ago. This time of year, it set early. Most people would be getting off work for the day. I chewed on my lip. Time had flown by, and we were no closer to figuring out my next move.

"Let's drive by. Maybe we'll notice something in person," Grace suggested.

We got our coats, gave Charlie an early dinner, and

headed out. We drove in silence to Victor's house. Grace fidgeted in her seat, bouncing her leg with anxious energy as she fiddled with her gloves. Finding out that she was also a witch had terrified me, but at moments like this, I was glad I wasn't alone.

"Thank you for doing this with me," I said as we turned onto Victor's street.

She leaned forward in her seat, her eyes focused on his house as we slowed to pass his home. Her eyes darted from house to house. "I don't see any Ring cameras."

I studied the neighborhood. It was quiet and peaceful. But in the back of my mind, the pressure was building. It throbbed behind my eyes. At any moment, something terrible was going to happen. I came to a stop across the street and looked around, trying to pinpoint the source of the sensation. A weight settled onto my shoulders, making it harder to breathe.

"It doesn't feel right." I gasped. I leaned as far forward in my seat as far as I could, straining to see into Victor's windows.

He crossed in front of the living room curtain. The wound patterns had settled even further. It didn't change at all as he stood in front of his bookcase, reading through the various titles.

"What do you see?" Grace whispered.

"It isn't changing," I whispered back.

Grace opened her door and strode across the street.

I turned off the car and darted after her. "What are you doing?"

She didn't answer. Instead, she plowed forward, taking the steps up to his front door two at a time. She knocked on the door—three sharp knocks that reminded me of a cop.

I scurried up the steps behind her and slid to a stop as the front door opened.

Victor stood silhouetted against the lights of the house. He stepped forward, a warm smile on his face. "What are you two doing here?"

"We headed out for dinner," Grace said. "I know it's impulsive, but I've been on a mission to learn more about my family's history. And I know how close you were to my great-grandmother. Would you mind joining us and reminiscing?"

"I could probably use a break. Winter is unfortunately my busiest season. Where did you have in mind?"

I stepped forward, looping my arm around my daughter's shoulders. "Slice of Life?" I forced a smile onto my face. Standing face-to-face with him was disconcerting. His face shifted back and forth from the cheerful smile he actually wore to lifeless.

"Sounds delightful. Let me grab my coat." He ducked into the house then followed us outside. "Ethan just took the van to the car wash. Is it all right if I get a ride with you? If not, I can pull the old hearse from the back, but people can get a little worked up when they see it around town for leisure."

"Of course," I said.

We all piled into my car, Grace taking the back seat and Victor squeezing into the front. His long legs almost hit the dash. We chatted amiably until we got to the restaurant.

Willow was behind the counter when we entered. She stepped out to greet us, her long, flowing dress gliding half an inch off the floor. I didn't know how she managed to wear her dresses in the kitchen without getting them dirty or tangled up on something.

Grace looked around at the photos on the walls as Willow scooped up a stack of menus. "I don't think I've ever asked. How are the photos organized?"

Willow beamed. She spent countless hours curating photos of the town. "Usually by decade. I'm running out of room, though. I think I'm going to have to expand or begin combining them."

"Do you have a 1930s section?" Grace asked.

"I do. It's the booth at the front."

"Mind if we sit there?" She turned to me, her eyes pleading.

I usually preferred sitting farther away from the door, especially in winter. The constant opening and closing of the door sent shivers down my spine. I grimaced as she pushed her hands together, as if in prayer.

"Fine," I said.

Willow guided us to the table. Grace claimed a seat first, her eyes bouncing from photo to photo as I climbed in after her. I left my coat draped over my shoulders to protect me from the occasional chill. Grace kept her coat and gloves on so she wouldn't accidentally touch anything. My eyes flicked to her. Maybe it was a good thing we were sitting so close to the door. It might look strange for her to keep her gloves on farther in.

Victor took the bench opposite us, admiring the wall. "You know, your great-grandmother wasn't that old. She was born in the forties. You might see your great-great-grandmother in one of these photos, though. She was the first Williams in Point Pleasant."

"I know." Grace smirked and gave me a little side-eye. "The women in my family have a tendency to marry young and have kids young too."

I pursed my lips and returned the side-eye. When I was her age, I had just started dating Ed, and we got married at twenty. In hindsight, maybe it had been too fast. Although, without him, I wouldn't have Grace. Imagining her married in less than two years made my heart clench. "And I am all right if that tradition ends with me."

"Did you ever meet my great-great-grandma, or did you

just know Melinda?" Grace asked as she studied the menu, which Willow updated almost every week.

"She passed away young. God bless her soul. It was only a few years after Melinda gave birth to your mom." He looked at me. "I don't remember much about her. I was so young at the time. But I remember she was the talk of the town for a while. It was almost unheard of for a woman to not only own their home but to keep her last name. Her husband died in World War II, so I never got to meet him."

We turned our attention to the menu and chatted about what everyone was going to get. It was hard to pick, so we decided to get a bit of everything and share. I ordered Nutella-stuffed french toast with bananas, Grace ordered a meat lovers' omelet, and Victor got the mushroom-and-mozzarella burger with garlic french fries. When the food arrived, we divided it up, so we all got a bit of everything.

As Victor bit into his burger, his face stopped shifting. I gripped the table. I couldn't keep the smile off my face. The visions of his death went away, and it was just Victor sitting across from me. I didn't know how, but somehow, having dinner together had saved his life.

"You look happy about something," Victor said.

"I'm glad we did this. I've been worried about you lately. Ever since... well, the break-in. I'm assuming someone broke in," I said.

He looked down at this plate and pushed his food around with his fork. "I've never lost a body before."

"Did they figure out what happened to it?" I asked.

He shook his head. "No idea. The only people who have access to that room are myself and Ethan. We didn't see anything on the security cameras in the hallway, and the only door that isn't covered, the stretcher wouldn't fit through. And well, could you imagine that boy moving a body by himself? His heart is in the right place, but I'm not sure if he's cut out for this work. You would be surprised how much upper-body strength it can require sometimes."

"Maybe he had help?" I asked.

He shook his head. "The sheriff already cleared him. He was with his roommate at the time."

"The victim's son?" I watched him over my plate.

He barked out a laugh. "I guess that sounds ridiculous, doesn't it? But it's not like they've known each other for long. They've only been roommates for a few months. That seems like a big leap to take for someone, you know?"

"You're probably right." I glanced over at Grace. She was only partially listening to the conversation. She was studying the wall of photos, looking from picture to picture as if searching for someone.

"I really appreciate the invitation out, though. It's what the doctor ordered. Food. Friends. I feel much better. I haven't gotten out of the house for something other than a pickup in over a week." He cleared his throat. "Anyway, you find any photos on the wall that interest you?"

Grace looked over, her face flushed. "Oh. I'm sorry. I can't help it. You know how we are." She bumped me with her shoulder. "We're curious to a fault. And I had never realized how much of my family history was a mystery until recently."

Willow stopped by the table to refill our drinks. "How is everything?"

"Delicious," we all said in unison.

Willow chuckled. "Any room for dessert?"

"I've got a second stomach just for dessert," Victor said.

She handed us dessert menus from her apron and turned to leave.

Grace leaned forward in her seat to catch her eye. "Actually," she said, "I had some questions about the photos."

Willow turned back.

Grace flushed again then squared her shoulders. "Is this all of them?"

Willow laughed. "Oh, no, I have a ton more in storage. The town has been so generous with their donations. I try to change them out quarterly, but I still haven't had a chance to show them all."

"Would I be able to look at them sometime? I'm trying to figure out our family history."

"If you drop by before we open, I can let you take a peek inside the storage room," Willow said. "I can't promise you'll find what you're looking for, but I'm sure I've got some photos of your family in there somewhere."

Grace leaned back, a small satisfied smile on her face. "Sounds perfect."

I studied her out of the corner of my eye. She had used the word *curious*. It was what I had said to Heather. *What is she onto?*

Grace looked over at me. I cocked an eyebrow, and she widened her eyes in a mock-innocent expression.

The rest of the meal passed, filled with companionable small talk. We dropped Victor off at his house then drove home. Grace leaned against the passenger door with her eyes closed the entire way home.

When we pulled into the driveway, she opened her eyes. She sat up and stared up at the house without moving.

"I don't know yet," she said.

"What?" I asked.

"I just have this feeling, you know? That I need to be looking backward." She turned to me. "I don't know if it means anything yet."

Grace got out of the car and went inside. I sat there staring after her as the car became cool. We were so much alike. Her words from earlier in the evening played through my head. *If I can't be honest with Heather, who can I be honest with?*

I followed Grace inside. Her bedroom door was closed, and the light was off. Charlie stood at the top of the stairs. He chirped at me and sauntered off to my bed. I chuckled and trudged up the stairs after him.

I had saved Victor. Somehow. And the one person I wanted to tell, I couldn't. *Why does being a witch have to be so complicated?*

CHAPTER 13

For the first time in over a week, I slept peacefully. I woke up before my alarm, well rested. Charlie did not appreciate me being up before dawn and had slunk into Grace's room for more sleep. I got started with my day early. By midmorning, I had completed two wind-damage inspections and was getting ready to head off to my third when a new claim notification came in over my phone. I read through the details, and at first, it seemed like a duplicate claim. Mabel Henderson's property had been vandalized. But the date was different. Someone had vandalized her home that morning.

I was in the neighborhood, so I drove over to her house. She was sitting out on her front porch, a giant mug of coffee clasped in front of her chest. She wore a plush red robe over silken pajamas and matching slippers. Her silver bob was styled, and she had already applied her makeup for the day. She perked up as I walked up her driveway.

"You here about the second break-in?" she asked.

"I am." I came to a stop at the bottom of the stairs. A basset hound that had been dozing at her feet lifted its head. Its muzzle was so gray that its face was almost completely white. It sniffed the air, let out a low woof, and dropped its head back down. Its ears flapped around its head as it slumped back onto its side. A second later, it snored.

"I took your advice. Seniors for seniors. His name is Winston." She rubbed his back with her slippered foot. He sighed contentedly and leaned into it.

"That's wonderful. I'm sure all the ladies on this block are going to follow suit."

"They better. Otherwise, I'll be picking up this ol' boy's poop alone. Maybe I should get him a dog walker? Anyway, I hate to break it to you, but you've come to the wrong place." She set her mug down and levered herself to her feet. She sauntered down the steps toward me, and her robe flowed around her, giving her a regal air. "The rascals didn't break into my house this time. They tried to break onto my boat."

"Your boat?"

She nodded. "I suspect they were trying to steal the thing. They took the keys for it the last time they were here, but they hadn't planned on me getting everything rekeyed so quickly. I paid a fortune to get someone out to do the boat on such short notice." She snorted. "But it's the holidays. I'm glad I did, or who knows if I would have ever seen my boat again."

I pulled out my notebook and jotted down notes while we talked. Nothing was missing, but someone had tried to take the boat last night. When they had failed to start it, they had pried open the control compartment and messed with the wires. The police department had put in a request for the camera footage. They were waiting on IT. Between facts, she peppered in gossip, comments on how cute my company's logo was, and complaints about the weather. A good forty minutes later, I was backing down the driveway, promising to find the time to volunteer at the local senior center. I escaped to my car.

I leaned back in my seat and closed my eyes. My car had become chilly while I was talking to Mabel. I blasted the heat, the warm air swirling around me.

I jumped in my seat at a knock on my window. My head jerked toward the sound. Hovering a foot away from my car was Gladys. She was a stark contrast to Mabel. She wore dungarees and had a smudge of dirt across her nose. Gardening gloves were shoved into a pocket on her belt on one side, and on the other was a well-used trowel.

"Can I help you?" I asked, lowering my window.

She glowered. "If Mabel doesn't see me talking to you, she'll talk my ear off at the next bridge night. I made the mistake of mentioning your note, and she has become positively obsessed with me giving you a statement."

I bit back a grin. Mabel sure was something else.

"So, are you coming in for tea or what?"

I got out of the car and followed her up to her porch. She stopped on the front steps and waved at Mabel, who sat camped out on her front porch. I waved as well and followed Gladys inside.

Her home was a mix of cozy and sophisticated. Much like Mabel, she had antique furniture in the rooms. Except there was something about the way they gleamed, while still half covered by crocheted doilies, that made them look loved. Fresh flowers filled a vase on the coffee table, and in every room, potted plants covered almost every surface.

I followed her to the kitchen. Large windows took up the majority of the far wall, looking out onto a sunroom. Cast iron pans hung suspended from the ceiling over a butcher-block island. Herb plants lined the windowsills. The scent of fresh-baked bread filled the air.

She washed her hands. "You hungry?"

"I could eat."

She grabbed a loaf from the cooling rack and cut it up

into thick slices. She slid a butter bell across the butcher block island to me and took a seat on a stool. I sat down on the stool opposite her and dug in.

"So, did you see anything useful the night of the break-in?"

"Nope." Gladys took a bite out of her piece of bread and chewed thoughtfully.

I laughed. She had invited me in just to tell me she hadn't seen anything.

"You should probably stay for a few minutes, or Mabel will think you're slacking."

"Noted." I bit into my piece of bread. It was perfectly crisp on the outside, with a soft, chewy center. "Have you lived here long?"

Gladys shrugged. "Yes, and no. I grew up in this house but moved out when I was twenty. When my mom got sick a few years ago, I moved back in, and she left it to me when she passed."

"Sounds like you've got a lot of history here."

"I do. Most of these plants were my mom's. I took after her. Green thumb wise anyway."

I broke off another piece of my bread slice and coated it with butter. "I heard something about a dispute with Jim over a tree. What's that about?"

"My mom planted it the day my sister was born. She passed young. Real young. But it growing out there in the yard made my mom feel like she was still around. It's got sentimental value." She pointed out her window at a large willow tree in the yard. Its wide branch umbrella hung over most of her yard, as well as a large section of the Mitchell's yard.

"It's beautiful," I said.

"I think so. Jim wasn't a fan. But he was coming around."

"Really?" I asked.

"In a roundabout way." She broke off another piece of bread and slathered on more butter. Her movements were quick and sharp. "We were so close to coming to an agreement on it. One more conversation, and we would have had the deal signed. And now I'm back to step one with his son. Or that charity. Whoever I need to talk to, I'm back at the beginning again."

"I'm sorry. Hopefully, they will be as open-minded as Jim."

"It wasn't that he was open-minded." She waved her hand toward the tree. "He just needed the money and was willing to sell me a piece of his land to get it."

My jaw dropped. *He needed money?* "I thought he was... well off?"

"He was. Just not in a way that was easy to access quickly. He was so desperate to buy out his partner that he was willing to sell to me."

I shook my head. Alex moved up to the top of my suspect list. An impending buyout wouldn't be good for him. At least, I didn't think it would. Buyouts weren't things that happened when everything was going well.

"Did he ever say why he wanted to buy Alex out?" I asked.

"Nope. Didn't ask. I just wanted to make sure my sister's tree got to continue growing." She peeked outside. Mabel had gone inside. "Looks like we talked long enough."

"Thanks for the bread."

She walked me to the door. I went straight to my car, my head buzzing with the news. That could be the breakthrough I had been looking for. I tossed myself into the front seat and stopped. *Victor is fine now. Why do I still care?* It was because of the dream, which was hard to shake, but an experience like that made it feel like my responsibility.

I pulled out my phone and dialed Heather out of habit. She picked up on the fourth ring.

"You won't believe what I just found out," I said.

I was greeted with silence. After a few seconds, she sighed. "What did you find out?"

"Jim was trying to buy out his partner."

She was silent again. The seconds stretched on. "You should tell Chris," she said.

"I was just—"

"Being curious. I know. But unless you're going to come clean and tell me why you care so much, I can't support you. You're taking risks. How did you find this information out? Questioning another witness? Alone?"

I swallowed.

"Tell Chris. It sounds like information he should have." And she hung up.

I blinked back a tear. Heather had never been mad at me for so long before. *Maybe Grace is right, and I should tell her? Will she still like me if she knows I'm a witch?* I stared at my phone in my hands and followed Heather's advice and called Chris.

"You got time for lunch?" I asked.

"I'm on patrol. I've got a PB and J I could share," he said.

"How about I stop and pick up something a bit more robust?"

He gave me his order for Abby's bistro. I picked it up on my way to meet him at the crossroads at the edge of Miller's farm. He lit up when I got out of my car with a to-go bag in hand. I took a seat in the car next to him.

"You spoil me." He beamed as he ripped open the bag. Inside was a steaming bowl of chili with jalapeno cornbread on the side.

"How's the case going?" I asked.

He gave me a sidelong glance as he tore the cornbread into pieces to dunk into the chili. "Slowly. No one has a bad word to say about Jim. It makes it hard to come up with leads."

"I spoke with some of his neighbors today." I followed suit

and dunked a piece of cornbread into my chili. I balanced the bowl on my knees as I scooped beans onto the bread.

"What were you doing that for? You aren't investigating again, are you?"

"Maybe a little." I ducked my head. "But it's related to my work again, I swear. I got a claim for a break-in at the Palmer residence. They're neighbors. I can't help it if retired women like to gossip."

"And what gossip did they bring to you this time?" he asked.

"Jim was trying to buy Alex out."

He turned his head to me, his eyes wide. "That's some gossip."

"Useful gossip?" I smiled and bumped my shoulder against his.

"Potentially. Alex didn't mention that at all when we spoke. But why kill the woman? He didn't know her."

My smile widened. Two pieces of gossip in one day. "They did. The woman? She and Jim were getting friendly online. And I think Alex was paying her to do it. I saw them talking at the diner. She said he was behind on his payments."

Chris's eyes widened further.

"So, it is useful gossip?"

He nodded.

"Great. So obviously we need to talk to him about it," I said, as I finished my bowl of chili. I wiped the last piece of bread along the bottom of the bowl, soaking up each precious drop.

"We?" he spluttered, almost spitting out his last bite.

"Yes, we." I poked him in the ribs. "I brought the gossip. I get to see where it leads."

"Bob isn't going to like that."

"I could just go talk to him on my own." I fluttered my eyelashes at him.

"Absolutely not." He shoved the bowl back into the to-go

bag. "Fine. You can come. But no questions. You just happen to be there with me. Got it?"

"Deal." I held out my hand.

We shook on it, a wry smile on his lips. "Don't make me regret this. Now get in."

CHAPTER 14

We left my car parked in the small corner lot and drove into town together. I held Chris's hand, our fingers intertwined. He understood my need to know. Curiosity had driven him into law enforcement. It was one thing we had in common. My stomach fluttered as he ran his thumb against the back of my hand. Investigating together was almost like a date. Almost.

The drive into town wasn't long enough. I enjoyed every second of us holding hands and couldn't help my disappointment when we parked in front of Mitchell Real Estate. It was only a few doors down from my office in a building original to the Point Pleasant founding. It took up all three floors of the large Queen Anne style estate at the edge of the harbor. I stared up at the tower that loomed over the rooftop. A placard near the front door declared it was a historic place.

The building was quiet when we entered. A woman sat behind the front desk, wearing a neat pin-striped suit jacket over a black pencil skirt. She typed away ferociously. As we approached her desk, she held up one manicured finger and spoke into her headset. "Is there anything else you needed, Miss Richardson?"

We took a step away from her desk as she finished up her call. Once she hung up, she spun in her seat, her bright-blue eyes roaming up and down Chris before settling, coolly, on me. "Do you have an appointment?"

"No." Chris flashed her his badge. "Is Mr. Sterling available?"

She checked his schedule before calling back to his office. After conferring for a second, she led us up two flights and deposited us at the door to his office. He had the corner unit, just under the tower. When we stepped inside, my breath caught in my throat. A spiral staircase wound up the far wall, and overhead was a reading nook overlooking the water. I stared up at it as we walked across the room to Alex's desk. I itched to know what the view was like from up there.

"Deputy Harris, I've got a call coming up in a few minutes, but I always try to make time for the boys in blue. What can I help you with?" Alex stood and walked around the desk. He smiled, but it didn't reach his eyes. They remained gray and cold around the edges as he studied me. "Ms. Williams." He nodded in greeting before turning back to Chris.

"Don't mind me. We were just on a lunch break together." I took a step back and stared out his window. I struggled to look like I wasn't listening as I studied the coastline.

Chris cleared his throat. "I just had a few follow-up questions. Have you given any more thought to what we talked about? Do you know of anyone who might have had any recent disagreements with Mr. Mitchell?"

Alex spread his arms wide as he sat down on the corner of his desk, splaying his fingers across the wood. "I wish I could help. In business, there are a lot of small things. Squabbles. But with most of his portfolio being abroad, I have a hard time picturing any of that having to do with what happened here. Locally, everyone loved him. And... even abroad. He did a lot of good. Low-income housing projects. Bringing solar power to the poor. That sort of thing."

Chris nodded. "We heard that there was talk of splitting up the company. Or maybe a buyout?"

Alex froze, and the smile slipped into a scowled. "Rumors aren't fact."

"So you were aware there was a rumor Mr. Mitchell might try to buy you out?"

"I was." Alex straightened. "But even if we had our disagreements, business is business. I didn't take any of it personally."

"Murder doesn't have to be personal," Chris said.

Alex walked around his desk and sat back down. "Murder is always personal. But if you would like to know, at the time of Jim's death, I was on a conference call."

"At five in the morning?"

Alex nodded. "We have business all over the world. Dubai is twelve hours ahead. If you want to talk to them, you have to make some allowances."

"And there is someone who can confirm you were on this call?" Chris pulled a notepad from his pocket.

"Of course. Dubai might be hard to get a hold of. It's the middle of the night. But an associate was also on the call. They can confirm. Linda can get you their information on your way out."

Chris nodded and backed away toward the door.

"Oh, and I'll be sure to bring this up at my next round of golf with Bob. He's usually much more polite and calls ahead."

Chris grimaced as we closed the door behind us.

Great. A friend of the sheriff.

Linda had the information waiting on a Post-it Note when we got downstairs. I followed Chris back to his cruiser and listened as he called it in.

Alex was on a conference call at the time of the murder.

A video conference call.

He couldn't have done it.

I reached out for Chris's hand. He squeezed mine, and we drove back to my car in silence.

CHAPTER 15

I studied Chris out of the corner of my eye. He sat hunched over the steering wheel, his shoulders rounded, as he drove. He still held my hand as we wound our way through town. If that had been Ed, he would have been fuming. He hated it when I made a suggestion that ended with him having egg on his face. Chris was just quiet.

"I'm sorry," I said.

"It's not your fault." He squeezed my hand again. "It looked like a good line of questioning. Sometimes good lines don't go where you expect."

My heart swelled. He really didn't blame me. I squeezed his hand back. "Does this mean your Miller Farm assignment will get extended?"

He laughed. "It's not all bad."

"Any leads on who keeps painting their cow blue?" I asked.

He shook his head. "It remains a mystery."

"That poor cow. If they can't care for it properly, it should be taken away."

"Not you too." He sighed. "That cow is loved. The Millers are good people."

"That's not what—"

The squawking of his radio interrupted me. Peggy's voice came in staticky. "Harris? Come in, Harris?"

"This is Harris."

"Abbott and Wright are en route to Victor's. The Steele body has gone missing."

I gripped the armrest, my heart skipping a beat. Victor had looked fine last night. *Was I wrong?* "Is Victor okay?" I blurted out.

"Is that Dani?" Peggy asked, her voice disapproving.

"It's my lunch break." Chris tensed, and his words were clipped.

"Is Victor okay?" I leaned toward the radio. I tried not to let the panic seep into my voice.

Peggy sighed. "Victor's fine."

"I'll be right there," Chris said.

"Sheriff Wright wants you to interview the son again. It looks like he might have known both the victims."

Chris got the rest of the details. The body disappeared sometime between Victor getting off work last night and noon today when the family arrived to ID the body. He suspected it happened when he was out of the house for dinner last night, because he heard nothing unusual all night, and after the last break-in, he started setting the alarm. Through the entire conversation, Peggy made snide comments about me being in the vehicle. By the time the exchange ended, Chris was glowering at the radio.

"So, you want to go interview the son with me?" he asked.

"Yes?" My voice shook.

"I trust you. I don't know why that isn't enough for them."

My face flushed. "Yes. I would like to interview the son with you," I said firmly.

Chris made a left turn at the next intersection, and we headed deeper into town. Brownstones and craftsman houses were replaced by blocky concrete structures. Driving

115

through Point Pleasant was like peeling back the layers of an onion. The town had been built up in rings over the years. The coastal areas were constructed in the 1890s, and the next big ring popped up just after the turn of the century. Farther from the coast, more and more structures had been built in the '50s and '60s. The son lived in the section of town from the '70s. Everything was right angles and had that dated futuristic look.

We pulled to a stop outside a three-story walk-up apartment complex. I stared up at the building. The paint was peeling, and the windows, covered with white vinyl blinds, were original. I followed behind Chris as he took the stairs up to the second floor. The metal banisters had a faded chrome overlay that was chipped around the corners. We took the hallway all the way to the last unit, which overlooked a decaying carport. It was a far cry from the elegant neighborhood Jay had grown up in.

Ethan opened the door. It was the first time I had seen him outside of his oversized coats. He wore a polo shirt with a faded logo for Tranquility Estates. Before he could say anything, Chris stepped forward. "Is Jay available?"

Ethan nodded and backed up. We followed him into the apartment. Two chairs in the middle of the room faced a large flat screen TV on the wall. An Xbox sat on the floor under it, surrounded by piles of games. Other than that, the room was empty. A true bachelor pad.

"He's in his room," Ethan said.

Chris nodded and walked back. I hovered in the living room.

"Can I get you something to drink?" Ethan asked.

"Water would be lovely," I said.

He nodded and shuffled into the kitchen. "So what's this about?" he asked over his shoulder.

He worked for Victor. He would know soon enough.

"Another body went missing," I said.

He dropped the glass. It shattered on the floor, scattering in all directions. He leaped back, cursing under his breath.

"Are you okay?" I asked, gingerly stepping into the kitchen around the broken glass.

He darted to a cupboard and pulled out a broom. I hovered over him awkwardly as he swept the broken glass up. His hands shook as he worked. He threw away the broken glass then hung his head, not looking in my direction.

"Do you know something?"

He looked like a cornered animal. I didn't want to startle him further, so I hung back a few feet. He peered up at me, his shaggy hair covering his eyes, and wetted his lips. "This is all my fault."

"What is?"

"He said he wanted to say goodbye. I didn't think he would take the body."

I stood still, my hands out at my sides.

"I told him how to get in through the back door." He was tripping over himself to get the words out. "He said he just wanted a moment alone. My dad died. I know how important it is to say goodbye."

"You told Jay how to get inside Victor's through the back door. The one without cameras?"

He nodded and licked his lips again. "It gets worse."

"Tell me."

"We weren't together that night. I know he slipped out just after midnight. He wasn't home the next day when I got the news. I had to call him."

The revelation settled over me. Jay didn't have an alibi. I slumped against the counter, and we stood there in silence as Ethan filled another glass with water. The water was still running when Chris and Jay emerged from the back.

Chris fiddled with his vest as he shoved the notepad back into his pocket. "Thank you for your time."

I looked between Ethan and Jay. Ethan was tense, with his back turned.

"Ethan?" I stepped in close to him and lowered my voice. "You should tell Chris what you just told me."

Ethan turned with his head down and his shoulders hunched. He stared at Chris's feet. "Jay and I weren't together the night of the murder."

Chris's hands froze over his pocket.

Ethan swallowed. "And I told him how to get into Victor's."

"No, you didn't," Jay blurted. "Why are you lying?"

Chris looked from Ethan to Jay. He straightened his shoulders and stared Jay straight in the eye. "The night of the murder, where were you?"

"I was…" Jay floundered. "I couldn't sleep. The bed isn't what I'm used to. The sounds. It got claustrophobic in there, so I went home. My dad still had my room set up."

Chris crossed the room to him and placed his hand on Jay's shoulder. "You know I'm going to have to take you in for further questioning, right?"

Jay nodded and swallowed. "I'll have to call my lawyer. Won't I?"

"If you want to. Grab your coat, and let's go."

Chris followed Jay back to his room. Ethan sighed and relaxed against the counter. He shook his head and stared down at his hand. He was still holding the glass of water. He handed it to me. "You still thirsty?"

I took the glass from him and froze. Everything about how he stood and spoke radiated guilt. But the feeling from the glass was ecstatic. My heart raced as warmth flooded through my body. *Why is he so happy? He shouldn't be happy.*

Chris emerged from the back, with Jay in tow. He looked at me and winced. He ran his fingers through his hair.

"It's okay. I can find my own way back to my car." I smiled

and sat the glass back down. "In fact, I'll call Grace now. She can come pick me up."

Chris nodded, and we all shuffled outside, leaving Ethan alone in the apartment. I rubbed my hands against the leg of my pants. *Why was he so happy? That doesn't make sense.* A shiver ran down my spine as I hit the bottom of the stairs. I looked up.

Ethan stared at me from the window of his apartment, a small smile on his face.

I hugged my coat closed around me and walked half a block to a coffee shop to wait for my daughter. *Why is he so happy?*

CHAPTER 16

Grace picked me up with only mild complaints. She dropped me off at my car then followed me home. I chewed on my lip as I drove. Jay didn't have an alibi. That should have been the big break in the case, but the tension in my shoulders and the pressure at the back of my eyes told me otherwise. I parked in the driveway, shuffled to the porch, and took the stairs up to the house in a daze. The moment Ethan handed me the glass replayed in my head. There was a mismatch between how he was acting and how he was feeling. *But why?*

I tripped over a package near the front door. Pain shot up my leg as my toes hit the front of my boots. I hopped up and down as I shook out my leg.

"Are you okay?" Grace asked.

I bent to pick up the package, and we continued inside. Charlie launched himself at my legs, pushing his body into me and purring. I scooped him up in one arm and carried him and the package into the kitchen. I froze in the doorway.

Scattered across every surface were photos and yellowed paper. I deposited the package and the cat onto a stool and picked up the closest photo. It was a grainy shot of a man standing next to a Model T car. "What's all this?"

"Photos." Grace snatched it from my hand and returned it to the stack. "Willow let me borrow a few boxes."

"Why?"

"There were too many to look through before she opened. I'm going to bring them back." She turned and crossed her arms. "How's the case going?"

"I could use some tea before talking about that," I said, resting my hip against the counter.

"That bad, huh?" She filled the kettle with water.

"In theory, we just had a big breakthrough." I sighed and pinched the bridge of my nose. "It doesn't feel right, though. I feel like I'm missing something."

"What do you normally do when you're missing something?"

I shrugged. "Talk it out."

"With Heather?" She peeked at me over her shoulder as she readied the mugs.

I hugged my arms to myself. "She didn't want to talk last time I spoke to her."

"Have you told her yet?"

I shifted under her gaze. I groped around, trying to find something else to talk about. My eyes landed on the package, and I picked it up. "Did you order something?"

"I thought you did. Maybe it's a Christmas present."

I shook my head, turning the package over in my hands. It was wrapped in brown paper, sealed shut with layers of tape, and addressed to me. The handwriting was in big blocky letters, written in Sharpie. I ran my fingers over the words. I inhaled deeply, my lungs expanding to their fullest. My spine straightened. I ran my fingers over the words again. There was an emotional residue there. I handed the package to Grace. "What do you think?"

She looked up at me and pulled off her gloves. She ran her fingers over the letters. "Pride?"

I nodded, and she handed the package back to me. She

121

put the gloves back on and wrapped her arms around her body.

"And no return address," she added.

We stared at the package. She handed me a knife from the drawer, and I slipped it under the tape. I tore the corner of the brown paper. My hands shook as the corner of a leather-bound notebook came free from the paper.

I looked up, and we held each other's gaze. It was another notebook from my gran. I tore off the rest of the packaging. My hands shook as I opened the book. Grace came to stand next to me as we flipped through the pages. With the last two books, there had been letters from my gran but not with this one. The pages were filled with her tiny script, each word neat and orderly. On the last page, in the bottom corner, it said, "4 of 7."

I blinked.

Four of seven?

"It came out of order," Grace whispered. "Why?"

"I don't know."

The kettle screeched. Grace flinched and darted to turn off the kettle. She made us tea, and we carried the notebook into the living room so we could sit next to each other on the couch. Charlie hopped up next to us and climbed onto the back of the couch. He sat perched between our shoulders, staring down at the book as we slowly thumbed through the pages. It was an entire notebook on Transmutation. We skimmed through each of the spells.

"I'm not sure how useful that one's going to be." Grace pointed to a spell halfway through the book. It changed a solid back into a liquid but only while the spell was active. "Maybe if you really needed water?"

"Could be useful for defrosting your car in the morning." I flipped to the next page. At the top of the page, it said *Restore*. I read through the spell, my smile spreading wider and wider on my face the farther I got. It was a spell that fixed broken items.

Grace wrapped her arm around me. She was radiating the same giddy energy. "This is it. You could fix the crab and look back at the murder. We have to practice it."

We jumped up from the couch and ran to gather the needed items. Charlie scampered around our feet, chirping with enthusiasm. I rifled through our baking supplies. The spell required some sort of natural glue, and it listed a few examples—beeswax, tree sap, or cornstarch. Tucked away in the back corner was a yellow can of cornstarch. Grace went to her room and emerged a few minutes later with a hairbrush. The head of it had broken off in her thick hair.

We cleared off a section of the kitchen counter and spread out the pieces. On one side, we placed the notebook. On the other side, we put a small bowl with cornstarch in it. The hairbrush went in the middle. I poured a tablespoon of water into the cornstarch and stirred it until it became a thick paste.

"You ready?" She hovered a foot away from me.

I nodded and shook out my arms. I read through the spell one last time then bowed my head over the bowl of cornstarch. I whispered the words to the spell, my eyes focused on the page. Motes of light floated out of my mouth. Grace gasped behind me. I faltered, and the light dissipated.

"What?" I asked.

"I… I haven't seen you do magic before." She covered her mouth with her hand, her eyes glistening. "It's beautiful."

"You can see it?"

She nodded.

I shook myself again and turned my head back to the bowl. My stomach fluttered. I had never had an audience before. At least not one who could see the magic. *Would I be able to see hers?* I pushed the thought out of my mind and focused on the words. Motes of light escaped my lips as I whispered the words of the spell again. They fluttered through the air before settling over the cornstarch. Once the paste was glowing, I scooped a portion of it out and spread it across the broken end of the brush. I fumbled with the brush, trying to keep the notebook in sight as I coated one of the broken ends.

I continued whispering the words to the spell as I worked. The lights swirled between me, the paste, and the brush. I pushed the two ends of the broken brush together and said the last words of the spell. The lights settled into the brush, and it glowed brightly, the jagged edge of the break shone the brightest. I squinted against the light.

After a few seconds, the light faded. I blinked, clearing the dots from my vision. The brush was whole.

I turned it over in my hands. All signs of the cornstarch were gone from the handle. It looked like it had never broken. Grinning, I handed the brush to Grace.

"It worked." She looked from me to the brush and back again.

"It worked."

She squealed and gripped me by my arms. We jumped around the kitchen, saying, "It worked" in unison.

"Can I try?" she asked.

"Yeah. We still have more cornstarch."

We rummaged around in the drawers, looking for something else that was broken. We came up empty.

Grace eyed the brush. "If I'm going to fix it." She snapped it in two on the edge of the counter.

I took a step back and watched as she went through the same motions I had. While my lights were a gentle white light, hers took on a more purplish hue. They glittered and danced, sending small rays of light bouncing around the room. I stared in awe as she worked. I had never seen another witch cast a spell before either. Grace was right. It was beautiful.

She faltered on the first try and had to do it again. On the third attempt, she mended the brush. She raised it in the air, triumphant. I pulled her into a hug.

"We did it." She clung to me as we danced around the kitchen.

Charlie leaped around between our feet, gracefully avoiding getting tangled up in our legs.

We broke apart, wide smiles on our faces. I stumbled out into the living room and collapsed on the couch.

"You know what this calls for?" Grace called from the kitchen.

"What?"

"Celebratory hot chocolate!" She filled the kettle again.

I curled up on the couch. Charlie slipped into my lap. A few minutes later, Grace joined me, and we sat, sipping our hot chocolates and giggling over our first successful spell together.

"Mom?" Grace sank into my side, her head on my shoulder. "Thanks for being there for me when I had to drop out of school. Dad just… couldn't get it like you do. I'm really glad I moved in with you."

I wrapped my arm around her. "Me too."

CHAPTER 17

The next morning, I rose before dawn and slipped out of the house. The spell had been a resounding success, but when I'd crawled into bed to sleep, the uncertainty of the day had clung to me. I was missing something. Ethan shouldn't have been happy about his roommate being taken in for questioning.

The fight with Heather wasn't sitting well either. I drove to the pier, the jar of cornstarch and the newest journal from my gran stashed in my purse. I parked at the entrance of the pier and sat there, staring blindly forward. It was well before dawn, but Heather would already be up, prepping for the day. She baked all of her own cookies and cupcakes, and she always woke up early to get started. It was time for me to be honest with her. The butterflies in my stomach did somersaults. I pulled out my phone and punched in her number.

"Could you meet me at the pier?" I asked when she answered.

"Why?"

"I owe you an explanation. And it would be easier here." I held my breath, waiting for her to answer.

"I've got to get these cookies out of the oven, and then I'll be over."

I fidgeted in my seat as I waited. A dark layer of clouds covered the sky, and a thick fog was rolling in from the sound. The streetlights looked like glowing orbs in the darkness. The minutes ticketed by. I got out the notebook and rechecked it and the cornstarch. I was fiddling with the container for the fourth time when Heather walked up and tapped on my window.

I got out, pulling my coat closed around me. Heather hugged her jacket to her body. She looked away from me, her shoulders hunched. I shifted my weight from foot to foot.

"Thank you for coming," I said.

Heather looked at me. Her eyes were puffy. "It's probably foolish of me, but you know I'm always going to come, right?"

I nodded and swallowed, my mouth going dry. The muscles in my legs quivered. "I've got something to show you. Can you just... humor me for a few minutes?"

She followed me up the pier toward the Crab Shack. We stopped in front of the sign. It hung limply. The tear had widened and almost reached the bottom of the poster.

"Could you hold the pieces together?" I asked her.

She gave me a quizzical look but obliged. She lined up the parts and held them up at eye level. "Okay. It's a crab."

I fumbled in my bag and pulled out the newest spell book and the cornstarch. I took a small bottle of water from the bottom of my purse and mixed the paste together in the container as I muttered the words to the spell.

"What are you doing?" she asked.

I shot her a glance but kept mixing and casting as I focused on my intention. The words tumbled out of my mouth, mostly nonsensical sounds. Focusing my will, I repeated to myself why I'd come here. *I want to fix this poster. I want to fix this friendship.* The sticky paste clung to my fingers as I smeared it up and down the poster. It congealed against the tear. My eyes flicked between it and the spell book as my words came out faster and faster. The motes of light swirled like they had in the kitchen and settled over the poster. The light pulsed over the tear, and it vanished.

Heather gasped and took a step back. "How did you do that?"

"I'm a witch."

Her head jerked between me and the poster, her jaw working up and down, her eyes wide with astonishment.

"Grace wasn't lying when she said I have dreams."

She barked a laugh and covered her mouth. "I thought I was going crazy."

I blinked.

"That night at Tina's house—I thought I saw you change shape. This makes so much sense." She surged toward me and wrapped me in a hug. "Thank you for telling me."

I hugged her back. All the tension from the night before slipped from my shoulders. "You can't let anyone else know."

She stepped back and looked me in the eye. "Wait. Are you supposed to tell me? Are you telling me like a super top-secret secret?"

I laughed. "Sort of."

Heather stepped back and paced back and forth. "Okay. So what does this mean? You had a dream about Jim's death?"

I nodded.

"Then, don't you know who did it?"

"It doesn't work that way. I only saw what he saw. And he didn't see his killer." I joined her in the pacing.

We switched places back and forth.

"I feel like I missed something, though. Something important. Which comes to the second part of why I'm here."

"Second part?"

"This one isn't flashy. You probably won't see a thing. But... I have a spell that will let me see through that crab's eyes. I can look back on the murder. And hopefully, I'll see something."

"Wow," she said as she bounced around. "This is amazing."

I tucked the notebook away and pulled out another one. As I flipped to the right page to cast the spell, I munched on a power bar to make sure I would have enough energy. The spell flowed perfectly. I touched the crab's eye and watched.

It was dark, well after midnight, and the clouds covered the moon. Jim passed under a streetlight. He paused at the edge, staring out into the darkness. He turned back toward the crab and glanced down at his watch. A dark shape rose behind him. The person was shorter than Jim by a few inches. They swung a baseball bat at him. I closed my eyes and pushed past it, almost as if the vision were being fast-forwarded. Jim fell in a heap. The form threw a plaid blanket on the ground and rolled him onto it. Jim clawed weakly at his killer's arms, pulling one of the killer's gloves loose and scratching at their wrist, drawing blood. The killer kept their head down, so I couldn't see their face. They just hit him again then gripped the edges of the blanket and dragged Jim away. They both disappeared out of the light.

I blinked. That wasn't like the dream. I turned toward Heather, stunned.

"What is it?"

"In my dream, they dragged him away on my stomach. But in what I just saw, they rolled him onto a blanket and carted him off."

She chewed her lip. "Are you sure you saw his death?"

"Who else…?" I gasped and clapped my hand over my mouth.

Jim hadn't been killed at dawn. But Natasha had.

I hadn't dreamed about his death. I'd dreamed about hers.

"Tell me about the dream."

"It started with me here." I kneeled in front of the bench.

"And then I stood and walked that way. Something hit me from behind. And then dragged me."

Heather joined me at the bench. "Why was she kneeling?"

"I don't know."

We studied the bench. We both reached under it, slowly patting along the undersides and down the legs. My hand froze over a plastic bag taped to the wood. The bottom of my stomach dropped, and my heart skipped a beat. I ripped it off and pulled it out into the light.

It was a small Ziploc bag, and nestled inside was a thumb drive. Heather and I stared at each other over the drive.

I swallowed. Natasha had hidden it there for me. *Was she planning on sticking around? I was early. She could have easily been gone by the time I got there if I had arrived on time. Maybe she never meant to talk in person.*

"I've got a laptop back at the café."

I nodded, and we scampered back to my car.

CHAPTER 18

Heather asked a stream of questions during the two-block drive to the café. I barely had time to answer before she was on to the next one.

"I found out I'm a witch this year."

"Yes, I first got involved because I had a dream about death."

"I'm sticking with this investigation because of my visions about Victor."

She became quiet at that last answer. His was the only funeral home in town, so half the town had been through his doors when they lost a loved one. Almost everyone had sat with him at some point and had him help them through their first stages of grief. He had helped so many people through difficult times over the years that the thought of him being gone, of someone hurting him, stopped her cold in her tracks.

"Is he still in danger?" she asked, her hands clasped to her chest.

"Not anymore. At least I don't think so," I said, as I pulled into a parking spot. I reached over and squeezed her shoulder. "The visions went away."

"Do you have a vision every time someone is going to die?" She stared at me wide-eyed.

"No, thank goodness. I don't know how it works. Why do I get them for some people and not for others? I'm still trying to get a handle on it."

I followed her inside. We walked through the Bizzy Bean to the stairs in the back, which led up to her apartment above the café. Star greeted us when we opened the door. She looked around my feet then stared up at me. It was like a personal insult to her when I came over without Charlie.

She turned and walked away from us, her tail held high behind her. When I'd first rescued her from under my porch, she had been too skinny. Over the past few months, with Heather's love and care, she had plumped up, and her fur had come in thick and long. She was a majestic cat, almost solid white, with a single caramel swirl between her shoulders that ended between her eyes and a star shape on her chest.

Heather led me to the kitchen, which made up over half of the first floor of her apartment. It was massive, with an industrial-sized island in the middle. I pulled up a stool, and we sat, shoulder to shoulder, as she opened up the contents of the thumb drive. My eyes widened. There were over a hundred documents on the drive.

She sighed. "This is going to take a while."

"I have a laptop at my office. I'll go grab it, and we can split them. That should make it go faster."

Heather nodded as she slowly scrolled through the list. I jogged all the way to my office and back. After my experience with Marsha, I had put more effort into cardio. I'd had nightmares of her chasing me down for weeks after. Cardio still wasn't my strong suit. I wheezed as my legs propelled me up the last few steps to Heather's apartment then collapsed onto the love seat in her living room. She handed me the thumb drive.

"I took off the first sixty. You can take the last sixty."

I fumbled with the thumb drive as my heart rate slowed. The documents were a mix of news articles and court case documents in no particular order. I sat cross-legged on the love seat as I scrolled through the articles. I didn't recognize any of the names. All the articles referred to an incident that had taken place in Olympia, which was almost a hundred miles south. Traffic made that drive intense on the best of days, so I rarely made it down that way.

"This is all about the trial of Sebastian Bennett," Heather said after a few minutes.

"Same." I scrolled through another page of court transcripts. "It's a lot of forensic reports so far."

"I've got a witness statement," Heather said. "It's... graphic."

"What happened?"

"High level? Sebastian ran over a homeless man while drunk, backed up over him again, saw the man was still alive, and fled the scene."

"What does this have to do with the case?" I scrolled through a toxicology report on the driver's vomit. I scrunched up my nose.

"The witness's name." Heather stood and showed me her screen.

James Mitchell, III.

Jim? I read through parts of the statement and stopped at the name again. The language used throughout the statement was almost childlike. *Not Jim. Jay.*

"But what does this have to do with what's happening now? Wouldn't he be mad at Jay? Why kill his father?" I asked. "The news articles said they convicted him for ten years. Based on these dates, he should get out soon. He might already be out if he was on his best behavior."

"He didn't get out," Heather said as she plopped down next to me. She opened up another document and turned her screen to me.

It was a death certificate. Sebastian Bennett had died in jail a year ago.

I hunched over my laptop and continued to pull up document after document. Natasha had died getting these to me —there had to be something concrete here. There were more court documents, a divorce agreement, and some photos from outside the courtroom. I flipped through them two more times, going slower each time. On my third pass, I ignored everything in the foreground of the photos and focused on the people in the background. In the back of one photo was a fourteen-year-old Ethan.

I zoomed in on his face. He wasn't a scrawny kid. The baby fat had clung to his face. His hair was shaved on the sides and long on top, pulled back into a man bun at the back of his head. The ill-fitting suit was about a size too small. He glowered at the camera, his hands clenched at his sides. His mother stood near him, her hand hovering over his hunched shoulders. Rage filled every line of his body.

I flipped from that to the divorce papers. Sebastian Bennett's wife, Lorelei, had gone back to her maiden name. Sawyer. There was no doubt. Ethan was Sebastian's son.

Heather and I sat wide-eyed on the couch, blinking at our screens.

"You should show these to Chris," Heather said.

"These are sealed court documents. How would I explain how I got them?" I slumped back.

"You could send it to them anonymously?" She sagged into the love seat next to me.

We tilted our heads back, staring up at her ceiling.

"They think they have their man. Knowing Bob, they wouldn't even look at it."

She nodded. "Maybe there's something in his car or at their apartment?"

My head rolled toward her. "Why, Heather, are you suggesting I go on a dangerous mission?"

"No…" She turned her head and narrowed her eyes at me. "*We* go on a dangerous mission."

I stood and paced across her small living room, into the kitchen, and back again. "Okay, so let's say we do this. Let's say we break into Ethan's apartment. Then what?"

"I don't know. It's not like I've done that sort of thing before. Does he seem like the kind of guy who might take trophies?"

I shrugged. "I could try to confront him instead? Like I did with Brad."

Heather stood and grabbed her purse. She gathered snacks from her kitchen and filled a thermos with coffee while she talked, her voice going a mile a minute. "A confession would be good. He didn't seem that talkative when he came into the café, unlike Brad, who liked the sound of his own voice. Let's do a stakeout. Stakeouts are cool, right? We watch him. Maybe he leads us to something important? I don't know. I'm grasping. But we've got to do something. But what if following him around is useless? Maybe he's already gotten what he wants, and he'll just—"

I stood in front of her and grasped her by the shoulders. "I know. We have got to do something. A stakeout sounds like a great idea."

She swallowed and screwed the lid onto her thermos. "Then let's go."

We descended the steps at the rear of the building and got into her white Kia Telluride. I glanced into the back, where seats would normally be. She had removed and replaced them with shelves for pastries. It was empty, but the scent of melted sugar and cream lingered in the car. My stomach rumbled. She handed me the bag of snacks and drove.

We pulled up half a block from the apartment complex and parked. I had her park facing away from the unit, so we could watch it through the mirrors.

She raised her eyebrows. "How many times have you done this without me?"

I flushed. "Only once. But Derrick Miller saw right through me. You know how much of a perfectionist I can be."

She giggled and took the bag of snacks from me. She popped a nut into her mouth. "So, how many people know about… you?"

I shifted in my seat and stared at the mirror. "You. Grace. Some other witches, who shall remain nameless."

Her jaw dropped. "You can't tell me there are other witches and not let me know who they are!"

"It's not my secret to tell."

She popped another nut in her mouth and chewed it thoughtfully. She stopped midchew, her eyes getting wider. "Not the Retirees?"

I pantomimed zipping my lips and throwing away the key.

"I'm right, aren't I?" She exhaled sharply, a wide smile on her face as she relaxed into her seat. "That's wild. And Grace, is she one too?"

"It's not my secret to tell. You can ask her yourself."

Ethan stepped out of his front door. He zipped up his coat, hunched his shoulders, and walked toward the stairwell. When he reached them, he turned and disappeared for a few seconds before reappearing at the bottom of the stairs. He got into an old beat-up gold Ford Taurus with a red mismatched hood. Heather turned on her engine.

"Wait," I said. He'd taken the bodies for a reason. I chewed my lip, closing my eyes.

Do I stay, or do we follow? I focused on my body, noticing how the hairs on my arms stood up at the thought of staying but relaxed at following. It wasn't an exact science, but the Sight led me to places for a reason.

Do I stay? The hairs stood up again.

Heather leaned forward in her seat as Ethan pulled out of the parking lot. "It's now, or I'm going to lose him."

"No one's home." I slipped out of her car and crouched next to it until Ethan had rounded the corner at the end of the block. "Call me if he comes back."

"Dani—"

I closed the door and darted across the street. I glanced over my shoulder. Heather glared at me from her car, her arms crossed over her chest. I pulled out my phone and texted her.

DANI:
I'll make it up to you. I swear.

I jogged across the street and up the stairs to the apartment. My heart raced as I felt around the doorframe and lifted the fake potted plants sitting outside. I flipped up the welcome mat. Underneath, bright against the worn concrete, was a key.

I shoved it in the front door. The lock clicked open, and I slipped inside.

CHAPTER 19

The lights were off inside the apartment. I closed the door behind me and waited for my eyes to adjust to the dim light coming in through the blinds. In the center of the room were the two chairs. There was a TV tray next to the one on the left, with an empty glass on top. I slipped into the hallway. There were two doors on both sides of the hallway, opposite each other. I tried the first one. It led to a linen closet, half filled with toilet paper. The next door led into a bedroom. A twin bed was pushed against the far wall, with a dresser squeezed in between the foot of the bed and the closet. On the other side of the bed, a desk with a small bookshelf was wedged between the edge of the desk and the wall. I scanned the titles. They were all medical textbooks.

Bingo.

I moved to the center of the room and looked around. Everything was neat and in its place. A single notebook sat on the desktop, with a pen perfectly parallel to the spine. I took off my gloves and ran my finger across the desk. My brow furrowed, and my jaw clenched. The desk was an area of concentration.

I pulled open the drawers, one after the other, running

my fingers along the handles first before pulling them out. The long one on top held pens and pencils. The deeper ones to the side were half empty. One contained a big box of printer paper, while the others had miscellaneous papers from school. I flipped through them. Most had As, but there were a few Bs scattered throughout.

I shoved the items back into the drawer and moved to the bed, the dresser, and finally the closet. There wasn't anything interesting under the mattress, and the sock drawer was just filled with socks. As I opened the closet, I froze. On the top shelf was a blanket—a plaid blanket, just like from my vision of Jim's murder. I stood on my tiptoes and touched the corner.

Sensations warred with each other for my attention. My chest constricted as my pulse raced. My breath caught in my throat as I gasped for air. My knees shook under me. I couldn't breathe fast enough. Terror flooded through me. At the same time, a warmth spread through my body. My mouth became dry, and everything in the room came into a sharp focus. A smug excitement washed over me, chasing away the fear. The feelings swirled around each other, fighting for dominance.

Terror won.

I yanked my hand back, stumbling away from the closet. I stared, wide-eyed, at the blanket. It looked so innocuous, but I had never felt something so intense before in my life. I rubbed my hand on my pant leg. My phone rang in my pocket. I jumped and hit my head against a shelf on the wall. Cursing under my breath, I fished my phone out of my pocket.

"He's coming up the stairs," Heather said.

I almost dropped the phone again. I darted across the room and closed the closet door. My heart pounding, I stepped into the hall. There was no way I would make it out without him seeing me. I tried the door across the hall. Dirty clothes lay strewn across the floor. A large, queen-sized bed took up the center of the room. Keys jingled in the lock at the front door. I dashed inside the room and pulled the door closed behind me.

I shoved my phone into my pocket with Heather still on the line as I scurried around Jay's bed. I crouched down next to it and sat on the floor, just out of sight from the door.

Footsteps fell in the hallway, followed by something banging against the walls. The door to Ethan's room opened. The door didn't close again. I strained to hear. Something heavy hit the floor, followed by a few more heavy items. I inched forward to hear better. The floorboard squeaked under me.

I held my breath as the sound across the hall stopped. I picked up my hand to inch backward, and the floorboard squeaked again.

Ethan threw open the bedroom door. "Who's in there?" he asked, stepping into the room.

My hand landed on a wallet on the ground. I gripped it and stood.

"Sorry. Didn't mean to scar you." I held up the wallet. "Jay didn't have it. And Chris asked if I wouldn't mind swinging by to pick it up." I forced a smile onto my face.

"Why?" He narrowed his eyes.

"I don't know. I didn't really ask. Probably needed his ID for something?" I moved around the side of the bed and inched around him into the hall.

He frowned and followed me out. He hovered in the hallway between the two rooms. Behind him, in his bedroom, was a stack of cardboard boxes.

"You going somewhere?" I asked, taking a small step back.

He glanced at the boxes. "Yeah. Can't really afford this place on my own. My mom said I could crash with her until I find something else."

"That's nice of her. Is she close by?"

He shrugged. "If you consider Portland close." He pulled Jay's bedroom door closed. "Was there anything else you needed?"

My mind raced. *Portland. He's headed out of state.* I fumbled for a way to keep the conversation going. "When did she move down there from Olympia?"

"A few years back," he said, walking past me. "I'm thirsty. Did you want something before you head out?"

"No, I'm good." I hovered in the hallway. The hair on my arms stood up. I brushed my hand against it and inched my way down the hall to the living room.

Ethan wasn't in the kitchen; he was standing at the front door, his back to me. "I don't think I ever mentioned I was from Olympia."

I cleared my throat. "Jay must have mentioned it."

The lock to the front door slid into place. "Jay thought I was from Edmonds."

I took a step back into the hall as he turned toward me with fire in his eyes.

"Four semesters of drama. I thought I had it down." He stalked toward me. "What gave me away?"

I turned and ran. I threw open the first door I came to. It was the bathroom. I stumbled inside and slammed the door shut behind me. My fingers shook as I fumbled with the lock. It clicked closed as Ethan grabbed the handle. It shook as he twisted it, the door rattling against its hinges.

"I want you to know that I am sorry about this. I hadn't intended to have any collateral damage. But you and Natasha just had to stick your noses in where they don't belong," he hissed through the door.

I spun in place, taking in the room. It was as sparse as the rest of the house. A clear curtain hung in the bathtub. A bottle of three-in-one shampoo, conditioner, and bodywash sat on the ledge. I yanked open the medicine cabinet. There was a handheld shaver but no razor. There was nothing to defend myself with. I scrambled forward and yanked the curtain aside. Over the tub was one small window, just big enough for a person to squeeze through.

Behind me, the door handle jiggled and stopped. Footsteps faded down the hall. I stepped into the tub, took a hold of the window handle, and heaved.

Nothing happened.

I pulled on it as hard as I could, and it didn't move. Drawers opened and closed in the room down the hall. *What is he doing?* I looked between the door and the window. I froze when my eyes landed on the window latch. Someone had painted the window shut. There was no way out.

I scurried out of the tub and swung my purse in front of me. I rummaged around inside it, desperate to find something useful. Hand sanitizer. Lip balm. A set of headphones. And the newest notebook from my gran.

I pulled out the notebook and flipped through it as Ethan strode back down the hallway. The door handle jiggled again. Something metallic scraped against the handle. I flipped through the pages faster and faster until I reached the spell I needed. The lock clicked. I lunged forward and pushed the button again. I grabbed the plunger next to the toilet and jammed it as hard as I could under the door and retreated to the bathtub.

A metallic object scraped against the handle again. My whole body shook as I turned to the window and concentrated on reading the spell. I didn't have time to practice. I read it cold, straight from the book. Motes of light fluttered through the air before coming to a stop at my fingertips. I reached out and touched the handle. My fingers came back slick with paint. I continued to whisper the words, to hold the paint in its liquid state a little while longer.

I shoved the book back into my purse and yanked open the window as the lock clicked behind me. I scrambled up onto the windowsill, pulling myself up through the window as the door crashed open behind me. Ethan lunged and clasped his hand around my ankle. I kicked back at him and stumbled out of the window and onto the carport below. I turned and slammed the window down, releasing the spell as the paint touched down on itself.

Ethan yanked the window, but the paint had returned to its solid state. It didn't move. He glared at me through the glass, then he turned and ran out the bathroom door.

A moment later, the window to Jay's room flew open. I stumbled back. My hands and feet slipped on the slick roof of the carport. Ice crunched under me as I crab walked backward away from him. Ethan climbed out of the window after me, a baseball bat in hand. His feet slipped on the ice, and he threw his arms wide to steady himself.

My feet went out from under me. I landed hard. Pain shot up my tailbone. A whimper of pain escaped my lips. Ethan smirked and stalked toward me, carefully placing one foot after the other as he twisted the baseball bat in his hand. I scrambled backward away from him on my butt, keeping him in view as I felt my way to the edge. He inched toward me. Step by step, he closed the distance. I reached back, my fingers closing on the ledge of the carport.

"You should have stayed out of it." He raised his bat overhead.

A siren sounded across the street.

My head spun around as the bat came down. It grazed against the side of my head as he swung wide, startled by the sound. He slipped on the carport and fell next to me. I scrambled away from him, my eyes searching the street. Parked behind Heather was Chris.

Laughter bubbled out of me. Chris was here to save me. Again.

Ethan punched the carport. His shoulders shook as angry tears coated his face. I swung my legs out over the ledge and dropped the few feet to the ground. Heather ran across the street and pulled me into a hug. Jay stood next to Chris's cruiser, his eyes and mouth wide as he looked back and forth between me and Ethan. Chris had crossed the street, as well, and stood with his gun pointed up at Ethan.

"Ethan Sawyer, you are under arrest for assault with a deadly weapon."

Heather guided me back to her car and pushed me into the passenger seat. I shifted between laughter and tears. She closed the door, cutting off the sounds of the street. She walked around the car, sat down next to me, and shoved the thermos into my hands. I sipped the coffee. Its warmth seeped into me, releasing the tension from my shoulders.

I turned to look at Heather as she fumbled with her seat belt. Tears welled in my eyes. "I'm glad you were here."

"Me too." She reached over and squeezed my shoulder. "Although if this ever happens again, you are not going in alone."

I laughed.

"Don't you dare laugh. You have no idea how scared I was listening to all that."

"If I didn't have you out here, then who would call Chris for backup?" I asked.

"I didn't call him." She started the engine. "You just have some seriously good luck."

I sank into my seat and stared out the window as she drove me back to the café.

Am I lucky? Or do I just have fantastic friends?

CHAPTER 20

Heather took me back to the Bizzy Bean. There was a line waiting outside. She scooted past them, apologizing for the delayed opening, and ushered me inside. The experience of the day had rattled both of us. I moved through the café in a daze and took a seat at the booth in the back. Heather somehow shined when under stress. She became hyper focused on taking care of people around her. Before I knew it, I had a cup of coffee between my hands, a foster kitten on my lap, and a blanket draped around my shoulders, all while she bustled around to open the café for the day.

A stream of people came and went. I sipped one cup of coffee after another; a half-eaten muffin sat in pieces in front of me. The foster kittens rotated, scampering up my leg to my lap, growing bored at the lackadaisical pets, then launching off my knees to go play, only to be replaced by another curious kitten a few minutes later.

I replayed the whole morning in my head. Heather had accepted me. I had been an idiot not to confide in her sooner. We had found the killer. But the why of it all still confused me. *Why Jim? Did he see the name James Mitchell III and assume the father as well? Wasn't he in court?* I broke off another piece of the muffin and rolled it between my fingers before taking a bite.

Grace slipped into the booth across from me. I only half acknowledged she was there. My mind was still on the events of the morning. *Why Jim?*

She studied my face. Hesitantly, she pulled off her gloves and reached out to take my hand. Her eyes widened, and she yanked her hand back.

"I'm glad you're okay," she said finally.

I looked up at her. "Oh, sweetie, I'm sorry. I should have called."

"Heather did it for you." She leaned forward. "I'm proud of you for telling her."

I chuckled. *My daughter, proud of me?* It felt like a role reversal. "I'm glad you're not here to tell me, 'I told you so.'"

She barked out a laugh. "That comes later. Much later. Like, after the next time I do something foolish later."

I squeezed her hand and took another bite of the muffin. "I really am okay."

"Just confused," she said, staring at her hands.

"You're getting really good at that." I coughed. She didn't have a choice. Her powers to pick things up through touch were even stronger than my own. Mine ebbed and flowed, but to her, it was always a flood. Everything she touched, everyone she touched, she felt something. "You're right. I am confused. I don't like not understanding why."

She nodded and grabbed my purse. She rummaged around it and pulled out my phone.

"What are you doing?"

"You know who probably knows why?" she asked.

"Who?"

She flipped the phone around, a text already sent to Chris.

"You didn't," I said.

Text bubbles appeared. Chris was responding. I snatched the phone from her hand and stared at them until his response came up.

My fingers hovered over the screen. *Do I need him?* My stomach fluttered.

I dropped the phone and squirmed in my seat. Grace hid a laugh behind her hand. Her dark-brown eyes crinkled at the corners.

"And now I'm surprised. It almost feels like you want Chris and me to get together."

Grace sighed and sat back in her seat. She fiddled with a napkin, tearing the corner off it. "When my Sight started to come in, you had been out of the house for a few months. I was upset about the whole thing. Then I started picking up emotions when I touched stuff. It was rough." She tore off another section of the napkin. "But when I realized what was happening, that I knew how people felt the last time they touched something, I went into the old storage unit, determined to figure out why. Why you left. Why it ended. At the time, I thought something must have happened. And I thought if I could find out what it was, I could fix it."

"Oh, honey." I reached across the table, my hand hovering over hers as she tore another piece off the napkin. "It wasn't anything you did."

"I know that." She grabbed a piece of the torn napkin and tore it in two again. "I went in there expecting to find the why, and I did. And it wasn't anything I could fix. I love you. And I love Dad. And I know both of you love me. But when I was sitting there, holding things Dad hadn't touched since you got married, things that should have been filled with love and happiness, they weren't. They were just satisfied."

I blinked back a tear. I had known, but hearing someone else say it still stung.

"In the times I've seen you and Chris together, whenever I touch something after, I feel more happiness and adoration on those items than I felt on anything from when you and Dad were together." She crumpled the napkin together and tossed it to the side. "And I love you and want you to be happy. So... if you have been taking it slow because you wanted my permission or something, I want you to know that you have it."

She turned her palm up, and I dropped my hand into hers.

I held her gaze. "I am so proud of you."

She squeezed my hand. "Same."

We sat there in a comfortable, companionable silence as we wiped a mix of happy and nostalgic tears from our eyes.

Both the door to the cat enclosure and the door to the café opened at the same time, letting in a gust of cold air. Chris stood in the doorway, stomping snow off his boots. He looked straight back at me, and we locked eyes. He strode across the café and hovered over the booth. Grace slid to the side, letting him in. He sat down across from me, his wide shoulders taking up most of the bench on his side.

"You doing okay?" he asked.

"I am now," I said as I tried to hide my smile and failed.

Heather came over to clear the table. She plopped a mug of coffee down in front of Chris and a plate of baked goods in the middle. She turned to leave, but I caught the edge of her elbow.

"Stay a while," I said, scooting over.

Heather glanced back at the counter. The morning rush had come and gone. She dropped down next to me.

"So, how did the interview go?" I asked.

Chris looked from expectant face to expectant face as we all turned to look at him. "I suppose you have the right to know." He sighed. "We got a full confession."

Releasing a collective breath, we all relaxed into the booth.

"So he'll be going to jail?" I asked.

"Probably for a long time. We are still figuring out what charges to recommend to the prosecutor, but we are looking at least two counts of murder, attempted assault with a deadly weapon, two thefts and two counts of burglary, vandalism, and malicious mischief. Maybe more."

"Burglary?" Heather asked.

Chris nodded. "He realized that there was evidence on Jim's body, so he broke into Mabel's house and stole her keys so he could access her boat. He didn't realize how good Victor was at figuring things out, so he also stole Natasha's body, as well, before he could figure out the height of her assailant. By that time, Mabel had rekeyed the boat, so he tried to hot-wire it."

"Wow." Grace sank into the bench.

"But why?" I asked, leaning forward.

"He said that he wanted Jay to know how it felt." He shook his head. "That poor kid. I can't imagine what it must be like to have someone befriend you just so they can watch up close as they destroy your life."

"How it felt?" Grace looked from him to me and back again.

"Jay testified against Ethan's dad when he was a kid. He went to jail and died before he got out," I said. "I think he wanted Jay to know both what it felt like to lose a father, as well as what it felt like to go to jail."

"How'd you figure that part out?" Chris asked.

I fidgeted in my seat. "Natasha left some documents for me to find. Although I don't know how she got her hands on them."

"Corporate espionage," Chris said. "We dug more into her. Turns out she's a consultant that specializes in digging up dirt on a companies' competitors. We think Alex hired her because he heard Jim was planning on staging a buyout."

Grace picked up a cookie from the plate. We all followed suit and sat there eating cookies. After a few minutes, Heather scooted out of the booth when the Retirees came through the door, all wearing matching green tracksuits.

Chris cleared his throat and took one last cookie from the plate. "I should probably get back to it, though. Abbott is still learning all the ropes, and that much paperwork would make anyone go cross-eyed."

Grace kicked me under the table and looked hard at me then at Chris.

"Let me walk you out." I stood up and followed him out.

I trailed a foot behind him. We hovered in front of his cruiser. I wiped my hands on my pants and shuffled my weight from foot to foot.

"We still on for coffee next week?" he asked.

I nodded and took a faltering step forward. "I'm sorry I'm so bad at this. Dating me isn't going to be easy."

"Is that what we're doing?" His voice lowered, and he placed his hand on my waist.

I peered up at him through strands of my hair that had

fallen onto my face. He brushed it aside, his fingers lingering on the side of my face before he tucked the errant strand behind my ears.

"It's not traditional dating. Our busy lives make that difficult. But... yes? I would like to move past this uncertainty of what we are to each other. You're important to me. And I hope I am to you too."

"You are." He smiled. "Even though we haven't successfully gone on a traditional date, I would like to call you my girlfriend."

My heart swelled, and I inched in closer, keeping my eyes on his. "I would like that very much. Boyfriend." I stood up on tiptoes, my lips brushing up against his for the first time.

He kissed me back. The butterflies in my stomach took flight. I pulled back, a wide smile on my face.

"And yes. We are still on for coffee," I said.

He squeezed my hand again and took a step back. He folded himself into his car and drove away. I stood on the curb, watching his car disappear down the block.

I was still smiling from ear to ear when I stepped back into the café. Immediately, the Retirees swarmed around me. I walked in a daze back to my booth as they talked over each other.

"You look happy," Betty said.

"Do you have good news?" Agnes asked.

"Of course she has good news." Sarah swatted Agnes away and tried to loop her arm in mine, only to be supplanted by Betty.

"It's about time," Betty said. "So how was it?"

I blushed. I had been married to Ed for so long that I didn't remember what it was like to have a first kiss. My mind fumbled for something to distract them with. I wanted to keep that to myself for a little while longer. I slid into the booth, and they followed suit. Betty and Agnes claimed spots next to Grace, and Sarah took a seat next to me. My hip brushed up against my purse.

The notebook. I grinned and pulled it out. "I've been meaning to thank you for sending this to me."

"We didn't send it to you."

I blinked and looked from Betty to Agnes then Sarah. "You didn't?"

"Melinda didn't leave them with us," Betty said.

"Then who did?" I asked.

They exchanged a look, and Agnes said, "She didn't tell us."

"Not outright," Sarah added.

"But we have theories," Betty finished.

Grace swallowed and leaned forward. "I have theories too."

We all turned to look at her. She took a photo from her pocket. "I've been reading through the journals again, and my great-grandmother talked a lot about how the Sight is different for everyone in our family. You're good at looking forward. But me... I think my Sight is focused on the past."

"What makes you say that?" I asked.

She set down the photo. It was that photo she had stared at for so long in the album of my great-grandmother's coven. "Because this woman right here–" She tapped on the face in the middle. "The woman who wasn't part of your mother's coven when you were growing up." She looked at Sarah. "She's the woman I see screaming in my dreams."

I leaned back in my chair, my mind reeling. Every dream I'd had since my powers came through, that was connected to the Sight, had been about something about to happen. I had never had a dream about the past.

Grace fished another document out of her pocket. She fiddled with it as the Retirees whispered back and forth with each other. Their words completely overlapped, so I couldn't make out anything. After a full minute, Grace cleared her throat, and they all turned to look at her.

"I looked through hundreds, probably thousands, of photos in Willow's storage. She's in a lot of them. From the day they moved into town until May of 1946. And then she disappears. She isn't in a single photo. I went by the library, city hall. I searched around online. It's like she just vanished off the face of the earth." Grace unfolded a piece of paper and pushed it across the table. "Which brings me to this."

I picked it up. The paper was yellow and faded, but the black ink was still mostly legible. It was a deed to a house that was in Meredith Walker's name, dated February 20, 1946.

"And this." Grace held up a key. "I can't find any records of that house. It's not on Google Street view. But I went to it. It's still there. And I think, if I'm right and my Sight is focused on the past, if we get inside, I might be able to see what happened in that house."

My hands shook as I handed the deed to Sarah. It went around the table, all of us reading it before handing it back to Grace. Betty wrapped her arm around Agnes, and Sarah shrank in on herself. They sat shell-shocked, their faces drawn. I looked from person to person. The hairs on my arm stood up, and the pressure at the back of my head that always appeared when something important was about to happen built. It pulsed, stronger than I had ever felt before. I wetted my lips.

"What happened in 1946?" I asked.

Betty looked at me, her eyes haunted. "That's when our families were cursed."

Interested in receiving bonus content like inspiration character art? If so, join our mailing list and receive access to fun things like 'Foresight and the Fateful Ferry,' a free short story by scanning the QR code below. Go on an adventure with Dani and Chris as they journey into Seattle for a fun day out, and things take a dramatic turn when they stumble upon a dead body on the ferry.

Ready for the next bewitching adventure? Book 4, 'Hexes and the Haunted House,' can be found by scanning the QR code below.

In book 4, Dani Williams embarks on her most perplexing case yet. When summoned to assess damages at the scene of a wealthy man's alleged suicide, Dani's routine investigation takes a chilling turn as she uncovers inconsistencies that hint at foul play. With her keen eye for detail and unwavering determination, Dani sets out to unravel the truth behind the baffling murder.

Meanwhile, Dani and her companions delve deeper into the mysterious house Grace uncovered during their previous adventures. As supernatural forces stir within its walls, the house becomes a nexus of mystery and danger, testing the bonds of friendship and loyalty among the group.

Amidst the chaos, Dani's daughter Grace questions the Retiree's inaction against the Curse, stirring up unresolved emotions from Dani's past. With secrets unraveling and dangers lurking around every corner, Dani must confront her own demons while pursuing justice.

Join Dani on a thrilling journey of magic, mystery, and self-discovery as she confronts the ghosts of her past and unravels the mysteries of the present.

ABOUT THE AUTHOR

Eloise Everhart lives in the Pacific Northwest. Her childhood was marked by voracious reading and tabletop roleplaying games, fueling her lifelong passion for storytelling.

By day, she's a dedicated insurance adjuster. It's a career that has honed her sharp eye for detail and developed her inquisitive mind—a skillset she now seamlessly integrates into her cozy mystery writing.

Beyond her storytelling ardor, Eloise is a devoted wife, sharing her home with a menagerie of rescued cats and dogs who have found their furever home in the Everhart household.

ACKNOWLEDGMENTS

As I penned this book, I couldn't help but feel like I was one of the luckiest women in the world. I have been blessed with the support of friends, family, and my wonderful editors.

To my editors Rashida Breen and Stefanie Spangler-Buswell, you helped me refine my story, while making my words flow across the page.

To my beloved husband, Nate, I am forever grateful that you chose me. You stand by me, even through the late night revisions. You bolster my confidence whenever it waivers. Without you, I would still be on chapter one second guessing every other word. To my sister, Andrea, my father, Chas, and my mother, Tammy, your continued words of encouragement give me strength. I will forever be grateful for your love and support.

As always, I would like to give a special thanks to someone who is no longer with us, Andrew Henderson. I will miss our writing sessions where you acted not only as my writing partner, but as my confidant, and my greatest friend. You inspired me when I needed it most. Though we no longer tread the same path, I carry your memory with me always.

"Come on a journey with me."